Our Daughter, Who Art *in* America

Stories

By Mukana Press

The 2023 Mukana Press Anthology
of African Writing

Copyright 2023 ©Alex Nderitu, Christine Coates, Dennis Mugaa, Mildred Barya, Gloria Mwaniga Odary, Favour E. Ahuchaogu, Chioma Iwunze-Ibiam, Okoronkwo Chisom, Munashe Kaseke, Delight Chinenye Ejiaka

Published by Mukana Press
1200 Franklin Mall, Box 459
Santa Clara, CA 95052

www.mukanapress.com

Book cover artwork by Aaniyah Ahmed
Interior design by Ravi Ramgati
Cataloging In Progress

Library of Congress Control Number (LCCN):
Publication date: April 19, 2024
979-8-9896946-1-7 Paperback
979-8-9896946-0-0 eBook

Our
Daughter
Who Art
in America

THE 2023
MUKANA PRESS
ANTHOLOGY OF
AFRICAN WRITING

Mukana
Press

Contents

Foreword..5

Part 1

Our Daughter, Who Art in America..... *Chioma Iwunze Ibiam*.........3

Little Woman..... *Favour Ahuchaogo* 19

The Ripening..... *Gloria Mwaniga Odary* 29

Tsoro..... *Munashe Kaseke* 41

Market Craze..... *Delight Chinenye Ejiaka* 51

Her Name shall be peace..... *Alex Nderitu* 59

Part 2

She Lingers....*Okoronkwo Chisom* 67

Half Portraits Underwater ....*Dennis Mugaa* 93

The Way We Bend....*Milred Barya* 107

Body Parts..... *Christine Coates* 121

Author Biographies..129

FOREWORD

Two years ago, we embarked on a journey to discover Africa's most promising writers. Our debut Anthology of African writing was incredibly successful, being named a finalist in the Foreword Reviews Awards, Multicultural Short Stories segment, winning the Independent Press Award for Distinguished Favorite as well as the Reader Reviews Bronze in Anthologies. This reassured us that there was, in fact, an audience for Africa's voices. It spurred us on to discover more obscure writers and provide a platform for voices who otherwise never would've been traditionally published. This year, we received 564 submissions from 23 countries.

In this year's collection, we sought stories that explored the human condition, particularly stories that advocated for traditionally underrepresented voices. Within these pages, you will find an exploration of the human experience woven through the threads of emotion, discovery, and introspection. Each story is a testament to the power of storytelling, offering a glimpse into the lives of intriguing characters and the worlds they inhabit.

We started off with the intention to put out a collection that was an easy and light read. However, some of the submissions we received reflected issues our world is facing today. As much as we wanted a merely escapist anthology, we felt some of these heavier stories are timely, and they too deserve an audience, especially as war rages on in places such as Gaza, Ukraine and the Congo; Or, as the US and many other countries debate abortion rights, women struggle to find care. Some of the stories reflect our world. They resonate with depth, authenticity, and an unyielding resolve that defies the forces of oppression, discrimination and war. They speak to the universal struggle of women against the constraints placed upon them, offering a powerful and necessary affirmation of their resilience and unbreakable spirit.

We ultimately divided the anthology into two. Part one has easy-to-read stories with vibrant characters that will make you laugh and smile, and part two has stories that will ground you into some of the atrocities our world faces. We felt this distinction would better prepare our readers to consume the content in a manner and at a pace that best suits them.

It is our hope that these narratives will ignite a flame within each of you. May these stories serve as beacons of hope, resilience, and empowerment for all who encounter them.

Nyashadzashe Chukumbu

Munashe Kaseke

Everlyne Mosongo

PART
ONE

Our Daughter, Who Art In America

You see, I've been shopping at the bigger markets, not out of malice. Not because I am promiscuous in my shopping; It's just that the crampiness of this small flea market irritates me. Even now, I'm reminded of why I prefer the bigger markets. And I've developed a liking for the sudden blast of music, of marketing jingles, of the big market traders calling me Mummy, and hollering, "Customer, Royal customer. Won't you buy my fresh fruits and vegetables? They'll make you live longer." And we both know widows yearn for attention the way naked bodies crave for clothing, and I, Lolo Ezigbo of Umujioku, am no exception. So, I sashay over to their pyramids of bright red tomatoes and peppers, deep green okras and leafy vegetables, and tennis-ball-round garden eggs—don't get me started on the mouthwatering aroma of their smoked mangala catfish—and of course, I buy at discounted rates, just like you do.

Wait, did you just say, 'Oooh!'? You think I haven't found out that you stock your lockup shops with wholesale goods from the big markets and that you make a killing retailing them here? Ah, ah, I found out long ago.

So now you want me to hush about the huge profits you make from retailing groceries and household items and instead tell you about my daughter—your estranged goddaughter, who, by the way, I haven't had a chance to visit—in America? Well, I will. After all, we spent our childhood whispering secrets into each other's ears on our way to school and on our way to the Mmirindu River. I could tell you about Nkoli, but you see, it's a long, long story. And I can see that you have customers waiting to be attended to, and you're yet to bag the smoked mackerel and fiery yellow Nsukka peppers I'd like to buy from your shop. Don't forget to bag the rat poison in the pesticides and cleaning supplies section of your lock-up shop. Yes, even from out here, I can see the packaging with the green, fat-bellied rat leaping over a mousetrap and lunging for a brownish-grey chunk of bread. Or is that a piece of fish? Yes, you'll have to tie the items up in separate bags. The total fee is what? No, oooh, that's too expensive! You have to give me a discount. No wahala. I can wait for you to attend to your other customers, and I can see from your widened eyes and furrowed brows that you want to hear about my daughter in America.

I'm not sure you've heard this—I rarely mention it to anyone—this secret that has been choking me like a fishbone stuck in my throat, but I'm desperate to retch and vomit it all, so I will just tell it all. How long do I have left to wander the face of the earth, anyway? But you must keep everything I tell you to yourself. I don't want to hear *fim!* from anybody!

About my daughter, not the first one, Nwanneka, who died in the Dana plane crash over five years ago; no, that one was a high-flying banker. Isn't that how these newscasters refer to all successful bankers nowadays? Yes. I'm sure you know I'm not referring to Nwanneka, who, like her American sister, was good with money. And did I tell you Nwanneka helped me secure a loan when I was trading in textiles? True, we'd lost touch all those years—you and me. But can you believe that death can be so wicked as to snatch Nwanneka away from me? Nwanneka, who had a head for mathematics; she even coached Nkoli, her younger sister, your goddaughter, who lives in America.

So Nkoli woke up one morning and told her husband that she no longer wanted to be married to him, or to any Nigerian man, for that matter. Who does that? Only Nkoli. Only Nkoli would proudly divorce her husband because he wants more than one child, and she does not.

Yes, you still remember her correctly. Beautifully dark-complexioned and blessed with full, long, kinky hair! Too uppity to speak to you, her small-market-trader godmother, in public? I'm sorry; please forgive. But I'm glad you knew that she graduated with a first-class degree from the University of Nigeria. Ah ah! You really do have a good memory to remember my child so vividly. But did you know her husband was an eye surgeon? In fact, when cataracts threatened to shroud my eyes in perpetual darkness, Nkoli's husband, or rather ex-husband, swooped me to the teaching hospital where he worked and cut the cataracts from both eyes. I spent more than three months in their Independence layout duplex recovering from the surgery. Not once did I hear him complain about all the food and medicine I was consuming. Only God will bless him. But for him, I would be walking about with a metal cane and a guide dog that won't hesitate to bite me whenever I forgot to feed it. Can you imagine a whole Lolo Ezigbo like me, shuffling about without light in my eyes? God forbid! Anyway, it was this sensible husband that Nkoli followed to America and then decided to dump like a damp towel.

How did I find out? One night, the eye doctor's phone call woke me up from one of my recurrent dreams, in which Nwanneka strolls out of the leaping flames of a burning aeroplane, smiling, unscathed. And just as she opened her mouth to say, "I'm alive, I didn't die in the crash," as she has often said in the past five years. I jolted awake and pressed the answer button on the pealing phone. I heard a grown man sobbing like a baby. To tell you the truth, I yelled at him. I said, "What is it? Just say it, just say it if someone died!" To my relief, no one had died. But to my shock, he said that someone might die if Nkoli left the marriage.

To be honest, I didn't worry too much; I simply called Nkoli and asked her if she had forgotten to take her madness medicine the previous night. Isn't that what you'd have done? Yes, I trust that you'd have pulled your child's ears and talked some sense into it. But you know, children nowadays have a witty answer to every inquiry. You talk one; they talk one hundred. I filled her ear with stories of all I endured to stay married to her father for 20 years before death did us part. I even told her of the tears I shed when her father slapped me because I asked about the lipstick stains on his shirt collar. And yet Nkoli bristled, hissed like a cobra. Nkoli said, "Mummy, when it comes to marriage, quality matters more than quantity." Imagine that! She said quality was being in a marriage with Bon, her white American boyfriend at the time; quantity was being harangued to have children she couldn't care for. Quality was choosing love, and quantity was staying married out of a sense of duty. And as if this analysis wasn't enough, she reeled out some statistical reports my menopausal brain could neither fathom nor store. My dear, can you imagine being bombarded with nonsense talk cloaked in big, big English? In our time, didn't we know better than to expect romance and happiness from our marriages?

Of course, I told her to calm down and think about everyone involved. "What about Iyke, your son?" I asked. "Would he be happy with one mother and two fathers?" Nkoli hissed as if I had suggested that June was a synonym for July. Did I not know that Iyke was better off with one happy stepfather and biological mother than he was with two unhappy biological parents? My dear, she hung up the phone before I could ask her what happiness had to do with marriage.

Oh God, now I can't believe I'm crying in the market. Well, this is one advantage small markets have over the big ones. You can cry in this one and not worry about too many people shaking their heads at you in pity. In the big market, the traders will make a show out of selling you the handkerchief with which you'll mop your teary eyes. Phew! Enough about my daughter in America. Let's discuss the discount you promised to give me for the items in my bag. Just ten naira? Why not make it sixty naira? And why does the rat poison cost so much? Is it because its powder can be easily slipped into food? Or is it because it dehydrates and dries everything it kills? Fair enough. I just can't believe I'm spending so much to get rid of creatures that were a source of protein during the war. If only they remained in the bush and dumpsters and sewers... Anyway, I insist on a twelve percent discount on all items.

What did you just say? My daughter is in America; therefore, I have unlimited access to plenty of obodo oyibo dollars? Iyasikwa! That's what everyone thinks, but my dear, perhaps you haven't been understanding everything I have been telling you. Nkoli is what these radio presenters call a "vex-me-I-block-you millennial." Every time you have a conversation with them, you run the risk of being blacklisted. As I said earlier, Nkoli hung up on me, and afterwards, I called and called, and the mechanical voice on her voicemail would answer and start giving orders like an oracle in a shrine. Imagine that. Each time I heard the oracular voice, I hung up and cried and remembered how, after my husband had been murdered by armed robbers, I resorted to auctioning off my Hollandis and George and hand-woven akwete wrappers to be able to pay school fees and hostel fees and all the fees undergraduates need to pay to study at a Nigerian university.

Nwanneka was a second-year university student at the time, and I knew I couldn't afford to fund the university education of two daughters on my secondary school teacher's salary, so I chose early retirement and ventured into textile trading. And if you know anything about textile trading, you'll know that it isn't all Home Economics textile and sewing stuff. It is a dog-eat-dog world. Traders used to throw punches at each other because customers had been lured away to competitors' stores. Once, two traders punched each other on the muddy market path that passed right in front of my shop. Half a dozen traders tried and failed to pull them apart. They punched and kicked each other until one of them bit off their assailant's nose. Have you seen a face with half a nose? It looks, well, not just asymmetrical but zombie-like. Wait, did I say dog-eat-dog? Sorry. I meant man-eat-man. I waded through the marshy waters of textile trading to see my daughters through university, and this is what I get? I thought about this as I went about my business—mostly setting traps for the rats in my house because they'd just eaten the 'Uni' out of Nwanneka's varsity degree certificate and nabbed crayfish-spiced bread from the traps they'd outwitted—and then I would try to ring Nkoli again, because, you know, a mother never gives up on her child.

One day, I phoned her again, just as I was inserting the lost-but-found key into my half-empty trunk box of expensive wrappers. Nkoli answered, panting, as she said, ndo, sorry. She said she and her partner had been settling down, redecorating their house after their marriage. I looked at the receiver of the phone just to be sure I was hearing what I thought I was hearing—that my only surviving child had just remarried without my blessings and without my having returned the dowry to Dr. Sammy Yoyo. But I kept quiet because I didn't want her to hang up and blacklist me again. I sighed and said, "Congratulobia!" And she laughed her high-pitched laughter while tears stung my eyes because I didn't even know her new husband's surname, his family, or if they thought Nkoli was an orphan to be maltreated. Yet, Nkoli kept on laughing and laughing before she eventually handed the phone over to Iyke, who at that point was four, or was it five? Anyway, it was little Iyke who said, "Grandma, don't be sad." I nodded and turned the key in the lock.

The click of the lock accompanied the soft sounds of Iyke's "I have drawn many, many beautiful pictures!" I told him I would love to see them. He squealed as I opened the box, and I shrieked too, not in solidarity with Iyke's excitement but in horror at the strips of clothes my expensive box of fabrics had been reduced to. Half a dozen tongue-pink baby rats squirmed atop a bed of shredded Hollandis wrappers. Their mother scurried to the top of the pile and turned its nose up at me, baring its teeth as if in mockery of my empty nest. The phone and the once-lost-but-found trunk key slipped out of my shivering hands into the trunk box, and its lid fell. The locks snapped back into place. Who knows what Iyke heard in that trunk before he hung up?

I mulled this question for days because Nkoli's phone kept going to voicemail, and I didn't want to worry my way into an untimely grave. I reimagined the scene of the rats transmitting their otherworldly squeals into the Nkoli's American house, frightening Iyke into accidentally smashing the phone screen on the kitchen countertop. Perhaps I imagined this because I remembered Nkoli as a teenager accidentally breaking her banker sister's Nokia 3310. Or maybe I just desperately wanted to hear the voices of Nkoli and Iyke.

Then, one Thursday morning, I was driving to one of the big markets to buy a bunch of plantains and bananas from the local farmers. (You know the farmers only bring their produce to the big markets on Thursday mornings.) Anyway, as I drove, I swear, I was imagining the rats' squeals synchronising with Iyke's. I could hear them as I sped past the College of Education and the traffic warden adjacent to the Anglican cathedral, and then I felt my heart pounding faster in my chest and sweat pooling under my armpits and on my forehead. Sweat? On a cold and foggy morning? With the wind and smell of the night's rain blowing in through the windows, Strange, I thought as I gripped the steering wheel with my tingling palm. Just then, a rickshaw driver swerved into my lane. You know how those Keke drivers throw themselves into the middle of the road like those shell-shocked soldiers we saw during the Biafran War? And so it was that this stony-faced Keke driver swerved, without trafficating, into my lane, and, upon trying to slam on my brakes, I realized that my left foot wouldn't respond, that it just lay beside the accelerator like a piece of firewood. And my left hand was just a brown staff decorating my steering wheel when what I wanted was for it to blast the horn. Thank God for giving us the right hands and the right legs. Or else, how would we slam on brakes and horns in life-threatening situations like these? How would we send our cars to a screeching halt a spitting distance from unruly rickshaw drivers?

Truly, my friend, the devil was at work, orchestrating fatal accidents as early as dawn. And that Keke driver was just the devil's handiwork. I was about to give the useless man a piece of my mind when I peeked into the rearview mirror and saw that my left eye was drooping as if it was in a race to beat the droopy cheek and to save the droopy mouth from falling off my face. But perhaps the rearview mirror needed to be mopped, adjusted, or replaced. So I turned and looked into the side mirror and received the shock of my life. The left side of my face had simply ceded the registration of shock to the right side. This nonchalance reminded me of Nkoli's, and I just wanted to slap the indifference out of my face.

Even now, as I am telling you this story, I am not entirely sure how I was able to manoeuvre the car off the expressway and park on the side street beside Union Bank. I forget what that street is called, but it's near the government offices and the pension fund institution. And don't ask me how I managed to dial Nkoli's number because even that remains a mystery to me. All I know is that my right hand worked and that the phone rang and rang and Nkoli's phone—the miracle of all miracles—was answered on the second ring, and I cried, "Nkoli! Nkoli, please, biko—" but before I could explain, a man's baritone cut in and said, "Excuse me, please, who is this?"

What did I say? I paused to inhale and exhale deeply, even though death was knocking at my windshield. And then I said in my Home Economics teacher's voice, "This is Nkoli's mother. May I speak with

Nkoli?" The man exclaimed and called me Ma'am and said his name was Bon and that he had been dying to talk to me "for like forever." How odd it was that he would say that he was dying when, in fact, he was not, and I was. "Bon," I said matter-of-factly, the way Sola Sobowale would say it in a Nollywood movie, "I am having a partial stroke as we speak, and I don't want to die while on the phone with you. Please tell Nkoli... Tell Nkoli..." And then I began bawling on the phone. The Bon man started crying, too.

Can you imagine my daughter's oyinbo husband comforting me over the phone, encouraging me to call an emergency care unit or an ambulance? Through my tears, I said, "Emergency care unit in Nigeria? Iyasikwa!" Of course, I didn't say it in those words. But I told him there were no 911s or ambulances in Nigeria. Then I imagined a Nigerian policeman answering an emergency call in his guttural voice, "You're dying, and you can talk? Okay, send gas money so we can fuel our truck." And then I laughed at Bon's blind faith in the Nigerian police. I was dying, and yet there was some laughter left in my heart. Laughter strong enough to leap out of my half-paralyzed mouth.

And you go ahead and keep laughing like a yipping hyena. Go ahead, slap your thighs. I don't blame you. When you told me about your son in America, I didn't laugh so hard. Refresh my memory again: didn't your husband ring your son's landline and his Oyinbo wife answer and say, "Who's this?" and after your husband stuttered out his introduction, didn't the wife say, her face probably fiery yellow like the Nsukka peppers, didn't she say in her high-pitched voice, "Chief who? From where? Africa? You've got phones in Africa? Please don't call this number again." Every time I picture your husband correcting her, saying, "It's Chief, Eze's father, from Enugu, Enugu in Nigeria. Yes, West Africa," I just start laughing and laughing until my stomach hurts.

At least Nkoli married an Oyinbo man who's too sensible to hang up on his mother-in-law because she called from Africa. Now you're no longer laughing. Okay, I know I was wrong—that was an expensive joke. I am sorry, very sorry. But you know, it's fine to laugh when life exhausts you, and you realize that you cannot give heaven a karate kick. You know, you cannot come and kill yourself for your son in America. Me, I won't eat rat poison-laced catfish pepper soup because I have a recalcitrant daughter in America. Ah, ah, remember, I'll still buy the fish and the rat poison and the fiery yellow Nsukka peppers with its strong flavor and scent. Let's go back to my story of Bon crying on the phone and me hanging up and dialing Sammy Yoyo's number. I mean, shamelessly dialing it and thinking, my family still owes this man his dowry, and here I am calling him for help. Really, the dying have no shame at all—no shame whatsoever. Shame is a luxury the dying cannot afford. I held this thought for as long as it took the phone to ring and ring before it died on the no-answer beep beep beep. Almost immediately, my phone rang, and it was him, my favorite in-law, whose dowry we're yet to return!

"Sammy Yoyo! Biko, please," I yelled into the mouthpiece. My life depended on the call, so I screamed. Maybe I thought the volume would make up for the slurriness of my speech. If he listened with the phone held away from his ears, I wouldn't blame him for that. His eyes are already bad; he can't afford to have damaged eardrums, too. Anyway, he explained that he was out of town but would send one of his young doctor friends. So I sat there waiting, listening to a comedy skit on the radio. Oh no, it wasn't Nna Mehn's shift, although Nna Mehn's cheeky, witty punchlines might be what you'd want to hear as you faded into oblivion. Well, the comedian on radio was spinning this yarn about having taken a lady out on a date and realizing he couldn't pay for all the food she had ordered, snuck into the gent's toilet, and leaped out of the window, abandoning the girl to eke out the payment. It was a poor joke. He was what Nkoli would have called an innumerate comedian, unable to gauge the time between the rising action and the climax and the punchlines. His inability to count seconds in his head had ruined the joke for a dying woman. Or maybe the Home Economics teacher in me wanted to teach his character about etiquette. Anyway, Sammy Yoyo's doctor friend arrived with a backup doctor, and they whisked me off to the hospital in their car. Someone—I don't know who—drove my car to my New Haven Extension flat, with its decking full of bruxing rats and squeaking mice.

But, of course, the car was the last thing on my mind, as were the rats that had migrated into my three-bedroom flat. You know what was on my mind? Pawpaws. Ripe red, juicy pawpaws. Of all things to think about as you totter on the tightrope between life and death. But I kept remembering what that highlife singer said: this life is like a red juicy pawpaw. Once it falls, it shatters on the floor, spilling pulp, seeds, and peels, and the next thing you know, it's being shoveled into a compost heap along with dung and worms and earth.

I swear, my brain kept humming this song for my entire one-week stay in the hospital and even while I lay recovering in my niece's guest room. *Uwa wu Pawpaw,* I hummed to myself. I didn't have much to do but to hum and munch on the bowls of foods they brought: the umami-aromaed okpa, and ofe akwu and ofada rice and, oh, please don't make me go on. My niece, Irene, you remember Irene, who owns a boutique in the center of New Haven? Irene, who hasn't been able to have a child, although it was said that a boyfriend once impregnated her? But that's a story for another day. Yes, it was Irene who took care of me. Her husband is rarely home. The man has a rat-free mansion in Independence layout, and yet he rarely sleeps in it long enough to impregnate his wife. He's always flying in and out of the country, importing and exporting stuff. Irene doesn't seem to mind. She packages herself in designer clothes and accessories and looks like she's on a mission to enjoy her life while she can.

Watching Irene, I learned to stop worrying about Nkoli. I thought about Nkoli—for what is a mother without her child?—but I didn't worry about her. Not just because she phoned every other Saturday. Not just because she took care of my hospital bills. It was more that I was slowly coming to the realization that the children I birthed were not mine to begin with. I was just a vessel to bring them here, just the tunnel through which their train arrived at the station of life. Whatever hope and joy they brought me as I nurtured them, those were just inventions of my mind, made for my pleasure. It was stupid to give my children the power to chip away at the contours of my soul, to suck the sweetness out of my life.

It took me six months to realize all of this; the six months that it took me to learn to walk independently and to learn to talk fairly clearly. During these six months, my dreams of Nwanneka were radically different. She was never in flames, only in white dazzling clothes. And I began to wonder if I wouldn't be better off wherever Nwanneka was. Maybe I was too tired in my soul to think properly. And when I left my niece's house and began telling whoever cared to listen that I was a childless mother. At first, the oxymoron rankled and made my chest burn as though someone had rubbed raw Nsukka peppers on the red of my heart. But after a while, I professed this creed without any guilt.

And then, one particularly rainy July day, Nkoli called to remind me that it was Iyke's eighth birthday and that his friends were celebrating with him at one Stewart Park. Because it was a video call, I could see a gaggle of children stuffing themselves with pizza and candy and prancing about in their multi-colored conical hats. Two children ran towards the silver strip of lake in the distance, and three adults ran after them and brought them to the table where everyone was already singing "Happy Birthday to You, Happy Birthday to You" while Iyke fiddled with the ribbons on the cake-knife, itching to cut the cake so he could munch on a huge slab of icing. Don't ask me how a Nigerian child managed to develop a mad craving for sugar. Honestly, I wouldn't know what to tell you. But as I watched, I felt as though I was at the party in Stewart Park, that I wasn't alone in my house trying to get the rats to stop fighting, trying to get the rats to stop. Period.

Nkoli told me she and Bon managed to take time off work to throw this party for Iyke. Wasn't it wonderful, she asked? And I nodded even though it was ten in the evening and I was in a bedroom dimmed by a yellow bulb. Yes, yes, of course, it was wonderful, I said. "Look," Nkoli said, "Iyke made this enlarged drawing of you and insisted on showcasing it alongside his other drawings at his party." A ten-by-fourteen-inch picture came into view. This is what I saw: a coffee-complexioned woman sitting on a couch; her elaborately tied scarf is perched atop her head like a crown, and her crow's-feet-rimmed eyes are fixed on the yellow pawpaw-complexioned baby she is rocking. My eyes welled up with tears, and I felt anew the pride of motherhood, for I knew that Iyke had not just reproduced one of the pictures of me rocking him as a baby; he had added, somewhere in the wrinkled cheeks, the slightly angled neck and the baby's plump, slightly-raised legs, a sense of attachment, what someone younger would call love. But whatever it is, it certainly transcends love.

When Iyke finished opening his gifts and thanking everyone, he came over and greeted me on the phone. I was glad that he could say "Ndewo" and answer to "ezi ncheta ọmụmụ." I let him chatter excitedly. It made me feel hopeful that I hadn't lost all my children after all, that America hadn't chewed up my grandson and swallowed his essence. As we talked, Iyke told me about his hearing aids and all the dance videos he had made with his Daddy Bon. They both looked very chummy in the video call, especially when he kissed Iyke and said hello. Iyke tried to introduce him in Igbo, so he asked if there was an Igbo word for stepfather. I laughed because I knew what he meant but didn't want to help his mother in this regard. I told him to ask his mother. My mother, your daughter? he asked. I exhaled. My first impulse was to say that I didn't have a daughter, but my tongue stuck to the roof of my mouth. My mummy is your daughter, right? Or else you wouldn't be my grandmother. I hummed and said, of course, of course. To change the direction of the conversation, I told him to be good and respectful to his mum and dads.

When Nkoli's face appeared on the screen, her brows were furrowed, her lips pulled into a pout. "So what I have been hearing is true?" she said. "That you've disowned me?" You know how Nkoli talks like a stenographer's typewriter. No breaks. Meanwhile, somewhere in my pantry, two rats were fighting and squeaking and banging against my big outdoor cooking pot, my cauldron, and my bag of dried fish and rice. I considered taking a pestle into the pantry and pummeling them into rat afterlife, but Nkoli cried that I was snubbing her, that I really had disowned her, and she had to hear it at her son's eighth birthday party.

Did I even care that she was considering killing herself? Can you just imagine that kind of nonsense talk at her son's party? She said she expected me to understand that she was under a lot of pressure to work, work and work and pay bills and to pretend to be a nice black woman. Did I understand what depression was? Of course, I did, I said. But she didn't believe I knew. She said she'd been feeling like her soul had been dwelling in two places. Did I understand how hard it was to explain this feeling to a partner who would never ever understand? Then she sobbed and heaved as though she was going to faint.

Let her come home, you say? If she's so homesick, why must she suffer through the harsh winters? But you forget that she is doing what many mothers and I have done, sacrificing their comfort and safety for their children's wellbeing. When a fellow trader chewed off another's nostril, I should have packed up and left, but I didn't. I traded in textiles as the sewn nostril healed and the scars faded. I stayed because I wanted my girls to get university degrees. So no, I didn't ask Nkoli to pack her things and come home. And why would I, when I know that things are getting worse in this useless country and that Iyke won't get any affordable aural rehabilitation here?

So what did I say? I told her to stop crying because I could never stop loving her. Your life is like a red, ripe pawpaw, I said. Prioritize your mental health so you don't break down. You need to live long enough to care for little Iyke. I didn't explain how miserably lonely I was with her so far away, with her marrying without my blessings. I didn't ask why she hadn't sent me an invitation letter so I could visit her, if her silence had anything to do with the stress of immigration life, or if her marriage was causing her heartache. I didn't tell her she'd made me the laughingstock of Enugu and Umujioka. The timing wasn't right, so I did not. Instead, I bottled up all my emotions and wielded silence like a sword.

In the video, adults picked up their children and waved goodbye. A man with hair the color of cooked Indomie noodles yelled, "Nkoli, Nkoli! I need a hand with the cake." Nkoli wiped her eyes with the back of her hand and said she had to go. The moment the loud beep sound of the disrupted call died, I turned around and saw a very big rat. The gash on its head dripped blood, and a piece of smoked catfish remained clamped between its jaws as it scurried into my wardrobe, probably where its pups were waiting to be fed. I put down my phone and the pestle. The battle had already been won.

See how these treacherous tears are making a fool of me. A titled woman like me, Lolo Ezigbo of Umujioka, crying in a market stall? There's no end to the things a child will make its mother do. The child will make poor decisions, and the mother will take the blame. The mother will say, perhaps if I had forgiven them, perhaps if I had prayed novenas and fifteen decades of the rosary and committed them into the hands of St. Jude, patron saint of lost causes, then they would have missed the flight that crashed, perhaps their partner wouldn't have quarreled with them. Perhaps Bon would have forever remained in the gracious mood he was in when I was stuck in my car in front of Union Bank, battling a partial stroke. Perhaps if I had prayed more fervently, Iyke's hearing loss would have been reversed, and Nkoli would have arranged for me to visit her in America. But all these had-I-knowns are just irrational optimism on my part, much like Bon's faith in a Nigerian 911. Of course, I know that motherhood hasn't elevated me to Godhood. And I know Nkoli has her own chi, her own personal spirit, guiding her. As I said earlier, I'm just a vessel. But what is this vessel without its child? Or rather, what is a child without its mother?

I'm probably blubbering like a shell-shocked soldier at this point, but you know what? Life has exhausted me, and I feel like someone is massaging hot peppers on my heart. And it has stopped drizzling. So perhaps I should be heading home with my smoked fish and Nsukka peppers. You never know, Nkoli or Iyke or Sammy Yoyo might call me. And please forget about the rat poison for now. What? No discount because I no longer want the rat poison? Why? No wahala. Here's your money. Now you see why I prefer shopping at the big markets?

Little Woman

Iwas nine when I got into my first real fight. It was with the Okoro boys, a horde of mean-spirited children who made me cry once or twice a week. A poor imitation of a FIFA football, *my* football, was the bone of contention. The boys had claimed it as theirs and were inches taller than I was. They held it up far above their heads and tossed it to each other while I stood on my tiptoes and chased them around.

"Come and get it," the eldest said.

"Promise you'll never try to play football with us boys, and we might reconsider"—this was from the middle boy with two missing front teeth.

I had already considered giving up. The sun was blazing, and I was frustrated, angry, tired, thirsty, and sweaty from running around in circles. I had even picked up my sandals and faced the road that led home when Nedu, the youngest Okoro with dreadlocks and pockmarks from a recent bout of chickenpox, spoke.

"You could have gotten your ball if you weren't so short like..."

I didn't let him finish.

Mama marched me to the Okoros' flat upstairs minutes later to get my football. I trailed after her as she huffed all the way, her footsteps as loud as a herd of elephants tearing down a house. She banged on their door, landlady style, and a furious, red-faced Mrs. Okoro appeared.

"Ohoooo... I was coming to meet you and that thing you call a daughter."

"It is your children that are useless things," Mama shouted, "and I've come to warn them and you because it is clear who they learned stealing from. I want my daughter's football right now, and it better be as good as new!"

Mama was full-on screaming at this point, and a few neighbors were sticking their heads out of their flats, trying to catch wind of what was happening without looking nosy. I stood behind her, willing the ground to open up and swallow me.

"You want a new football? After what your daughter has done to my child?" Mrs. Okoro asked incredulously. Then she went inside to reappear with Nedu.

What I didn't tell Mama was that I had already fought with the Okoro boys, ripping Nedu's white and blue striped jersey with "Messi" written on the back. I had bloodied his nose and yanked away a handful of his locks. I probably still had his flesh stuck under my fingernails from the mile-long scratches on his arm. He was also sporting a bite mark on his ear and a black eye. I was outnumbered during the fight, though, and after his brothers tore me off him, they retreated with my ball. Nedu was standing in front of his mother, holding the remains of his shirt as she showcased his wounds to the neighbors who were already gathering.

I stood shamefaced behind Mama as they looked over the wounds and shook their heads.

Mrs. Okoro was loving the attention.

"Look what the daughter of this short woman has done to my son!"

Mama glanced at Nedu and faced me.

"Did you do this?"

Mama had never told me not to fight. Not explicitly. I wondered if I should have just told her that the ball fell into a big ditch or got stuck on a roof, especially with some of the neighbors looking at me like I was some sort of wild animal. Like I was the crazy daughter of a crazy woman.

I slowly nodded.

"Don't nod," Mama thundered. "Speak up!"

"Yes, but it was only because..."

"That's ok. You should have torn out every strand of hair on his scrawny skull and broken at least two bones."

I was as surprised as the neighbors and Mrs. Okoro, who was in shock with her mouth wide open, but Mama was not done.

"If I were you, and thank God I'm not, I would be ashamed that a girl did this to my son, and I promise you that I will send her to bloody his nose every day until that football is returned."

My football was sitting by the kitchen door two hours later.

My mother was short, a tiny woman barely grazing my father's hip in the old, grainy, black-and-white wedding photo hanging on the parlor wall. But Papa (and everybody else who knew her) used to say her footsteps were a contrast to her size. Even her bare feet sounded louder than my Auntie Grace's, my mother's younger sister, who was always wearing impractical, skyscraper heels and boots. Most people walked like Mama only when they were angry or when they were going to fight, but my mother walked to church like that, to the market where she sold foodstuffs, around the house, in the kitchen making *ukazi* soup—everywhere. To compliment her walk was also her famous stance—arms fisted and on her waist with her chest puffed up like Superman. Her heavy steps and her pose beside my bed were my alarm clock during my days in primary and secondary school.

Growing up, I always overheard—and sometimes had it said to my face, primarily by my neighbors and Papa's side of the family—that Mama was aggressive, too opinionated, strong-minded, and ambitious for a woman a little over four feet. They said she was overcompensating for her small size. I think there is a tiny measure of truth in those accusations. At her height, she endured the embarrassing feeling of people literally looking down on her, and she probably swore to herself that she would not let anyone do it figuratively.

When I proudly told Papa how Mama got my football back, he smiled and called her his *enyi*, his elephant, and I imagined my mother as an elephant and my father and I hiding behind her as she trampled on troublesome neighbors. But my father was far from being a coward hiding behind his woman's wrapper. Marrying my mother was an act of defiance against my grandparents, who, I am told, chose a more aesthetically pleasing and taller woman for him to marry. He was a quiet man with a firecracker for a wife, and so it was always assumed that she did all the talking. But it was my Papa who banned his brothers from coming to our house.

They had arrived from our village in Amapu to Aba in a noisy, rickety old van that used to be white. I was sitting on the front steps of our home, tossing my reclaimed football. Papa was napping.

"Good afternoon, Uncles."

"Afternoon. Is your father in?"

"Yes. He is sleeping."

"And your mother?"

"Yes."

Uncle Abuchi looked at the football, now tucked under my arm.

"You need brothers to play that."

Uncle Chidi nodded. "Football is a boy's game."

"I play better than all the boys on the street."

They scoffed and went in, and I immediately hid behind a window covered with black mosquito netting to listen in. Even at nine, I knew my uncles had more children than sense. They were both deadbeats, with not less than ten children each from multiple wives. They came at least once a year to ask my father for money and to remind him that he needed a new wife or at least a concubine that would give him sons. My mother would retreat to the bedroom when they came, but I was sure they were constantly reminded that she was close because her footsteps reverberated as she paced. They exchanged greetings with Papa, and he asked about the people of their homes and how things were in the village as if they did not just wake him from his Sunday nap.

"We are fine, just as you left us," Uncle Abuchi replied. Their faces were distorted from my viewpoint, so I had to press my face so close to the window that I tasted dust from the last Harmattan season.

Uncle Chidi cleared his throat, scratched his beard, and shook his head from side to side before he spoke.

"We are not here just to exchange pleasantries. We have had patience and waited for you and your wife. We have even begged God on your behalf. But it is said that heaven helps those who help themselves, so I'll go straight to the point: you need to make a move. Abuchi and I are your brothers, and we have happily gone through the stress of finding a young, nubile girl who will bear you sons. We have even met with her family, and all you need to do is come home for a few days. This is what we came to tell you."

Papa did not speak for a long while, and my heart beat painfully in my chest as I waited and wondered if he had fallen asleep. I willed him to speak, to be even a tiny little bit like Mama.

"Did I not tell you it would get to this?" my Uncle Abuchi asked Uncle Chidi. "I told you that that little wife of his is a witch. She has blinded him."

"Exactly. Exactly! He does not even realize that he needs help, and he does not even recognize a helping hand. Why do we have to remind him that he needs sons?"

Then Papa spoke in the same quiet way he normally spoke, like he was reading newspaper headlines aloud to himself on a Saturday morning.

"Leave."

"What?" Uncle Chidi asked in the middle of scratching his beard again.

"The two of you should leave my house. Don't ever come into my home again to spew rubbish. If you come here again, I will not be responsible for whatever happens."

Even from my position, I could see veins popping on my uncle's temples.

"Abuchi, let us leave. He has rejected our help and insulted us. We will never set foot in his home again! After all, he does not give us meat or *fufu*. In short, let this be the last time he sees us."

And it was the last time my father saw them. He died the next week in a car accident, burnt beyond recognition, I heard. Mama lay comatose on the sofa for days after his death, and I watched as friends and family trooped in and out of the house, even the Okoros. Family meetings were held, and a burial date was fixed. The day before the burial, Mama stood up, took me by the hand into the bedroom that used to be her and Papa's, and asked for my school bag.

"Are we running away, Mama?"

"No, just bring it. Bring my sewing kit, too."

I watched as she shook the contents of my bag to the floor: my exercise books, rubber bands, a friendship bracelet, pebbles I picked on my way to school, and wraps from candies I had illicitly eaten. Auntie Grace and I had watched a Nollywood movie where a woman went mad, and I was almost sure Mama was going the same way when she took a razor and slit the lining of the blue *JanSport* bag I had used for just a term.

"Your Papa and I always talked about how you are a child worth more than a thousand children. Everything he had is rightfully yours, and I would die protecting them and you. Do you understand?"

I nodded and then said, "Yes, Ma." Of course, I understood.

Mama brought out Papa's briefcase, upturned all the land deeds and our passports into the bag, and began sewing.

"This is our secret. You cannot tell anyone. Not even Grace."

I just nodded this time. I sat on the floor beside her while she sewed, her hands shaking and the needle piercing her more than once. When she was done, she hugged me and the backpack tightly, and we sobbed, my tears wetting her chest and hers falling into my hair.

My uncles came the week after his burial in the noisy van, and even Mama, standing in front of the gate with her hair in a black net and wearing the nightgown and wrapper she had been wearing for three days in a row, could not stop them. They took the *Toshiba* TV, the fridge, the generator, and my red bicycle, which Papa had bought me three months earlier on my ninth birthday. My mother stood aside, holding me, while she called her lawyer. Uncle Chidi slit the sofas and pushed down picture frames.

"Abuchi, look for our brother's land and house ownership documents. Those are very important."

Mama had left my bag hanging on a wall in my room the way it always did, and when Uncle Abuchi barged into my room, I kept my eyes glued to the ceiling, my heart beating as fast as it did the last day Papa saw them. They left, but it took months of back and forth between courts and lawyers, meetings with *Umunna,* and threats from my uncles, who were furious that "a woman no bigger than a rat and her daughter" were keeping them from their brother's properties. Mama waged a one-woman war, going all in and not relenting, not even when my uncles promised to use *juju.* She had Uncle Chidi arrested when he harvested Papa's palm fruit plantation. He slept in jail for days until one of his pregnant wives came to beg Mama with another baby on her back.

My mother lost a lot of weight, and her spare frame looked stretched and elongated, almost as if she had added a few inches. She used to wake up at night and pace, her nightgown slipping off her shoulder and her body casting long shadows on the walls, and when she came to tuck me in at night, she would hold me longer than usual. She drifted through rooms, her footsteps louder and hollow in the almost empty house. In the mornings and afternoons, she spent hours talking to lawyers and making relocation plans. Then, a few days after I turned ten, she got off the phone with Barrister Izuegwu and started crying.

"It's over. You are your father's next of kin, and these properties belong to you whenever you are ready for them."

In a new place, Mama was still Mama. For the past year, she had been in a house with the lights turned off, but in Port-Harcourt, the lights flicked on and off for the first year, eventually staying on after our second year. But it wasn't the same for me. I let the pidgin English-speaking kids in the neighborhood walk all over me. They were fancier and taller and had mothers that acted like perfect ladies. The girls were all wearing training bras by twelve while I spent all my spare time at the stadium close to our home, playing football with some boys who befriended me because I could juggle more than they could.

One time, at the public tap at the end of the street where we bought water, Tare, a girl in my class dared me to fetch before her.

"If dem born you well, put that bucket make I see. You think say I dey fear your Mama?"

"But I was here before you."

"You still dey speak grammar. Try me."

I did, and she flung my red bucket so far that it smashed to pieces. I didn't tell Mama because I was afraid she would make a scene and make it more difficult for me to fit in. So I told her I fell on my way home. But I think she knew because when she replaced the bucket, she said, "Don't let it break again," and I guarded that bucket with my life, telling Tare a few days later that the next time she touched it would be the last time she had a complete skull.

I am closer to forty now, with two kids of my own and ten acres of land that I do not know what to do with, and a husband who says I'm unconventional when it comes to how I teach our children how to handle bullies.

"Honey, are you serious about signing them up for another martial arts class?"

Just last week, I came home to my children stomping around our home.

"What are you doing?"

"We're being an elephant like you, Mummy!"

The Ripening

The day Mama threw a cooking stick at Kagonya was a November day so hot that the ripened bananas hanging on sisal rope from the kitchen roof were beginning to turn black. Mama had been sitting on a low stool, staring at the sufuria as the pumpkin leaves boiled off their green, humming along to "Cha Kutumaini Sina" on the radio. Baby, two years old, sucked on Mama's sagging left breast. I was bent over our blue bucket, washing utensils because the duty rota on the wall said it was my turn.

Our maid Kagonya had arrived with Mama in the clove of the season when the heat shimmered on the tarmac road. We heard a knock on the front door that we scurried to open because it was about Christmas time, and we knew Mama would be carrying a box full of Zesta jam, Tropicana chapati flour, and maybe even orange Treetop juice.

Kagonya had fit in so neatly at first. Like a slip stitch, she hemmed herself into our lives and patched up our torn. She got to work, teaching us to save mango seeds, peeling the skin of nduma tubers so thinly, and smoothing out our loose ends. She worked like clockwork, waking at four in the morning, moving noiselessly through every chore.

*

Because he slept on the sofa in the sitting room, my brother Kuka was the first to overhear our parents' plans to move houses. Baaba, a secondary school teacher, had received a transfer letter from the Teachers Service Commission. His new posting was in Kakamega, and we were to move into a big blue house in Amalemba with a toilet inside and a bathtub.

"I heard Baaba describe it. I swear, Bible red!" Kuka licked the tip of his index finger, then raised it to the sky. "Haki, our new house is not small and weepy like this one. It has a veranda, three bedrooms and a small garden."

I nodded excitedly. Everything Kuka overheard always came to pass. Like him, I wanted to spread my arms in glee at the thought of a new, bigger house.

Kagonya's mouth was a half-moon of scorn. "Kuka, how will your Baaba suddenly afford that expensive rent when his transfer is not a promotion even?"

"Because Mama says she will expand her fish business to support him," Kuka said, an impatient edge lowering his voice. Kuka was to be enrolled at Kakamega High School. His eyes shone as he spoke, "I'm going to befriend the city boys and ask them to teach me to play rugby."

Kagonya listened to us with both eyebrows raised. Having lived in Oloitoktok with her sister, she told us about town women. "Let me tell you. I made friends with salon women who hid their secrets behind silk curtains with embroidered borders. Their skins were fair because they used mkorogo from Tanzania to lighten them. One had hair that reached her buttocks; can you believe it? She used virgin oils and pomades to make that hair so long."

*

The hope of a bigger, better home lay before us like a guava tree full of ripe fruit. The games I played with the neighbor's kids had lost their fun. I wanted the days to move quickly, and Kagonya had a ready solution: "It's simple; the days go faster if you cut the tail of a monitor lizard and bury it in the ground."

The movers finally came, and we boxed up our utensils, wrapped our glasses in old newspapers, and tied our bedding. At the new house, the moment I heard Kagonya shout, "It's a white bathtub; imagine!" I scampered from where Mama had called me to examine the kitchen sink to behold Kagonya's call.

I stopped dead at the bathroom door.

The bathroom was covered with soft blue tiles that went all the way up to the ceiling. At the corner was a big, oval tub built into the wall. A golden swan-shaped faucet tipped its long neck inside the tub. When I turned the handle, it exhaled water as gently as a lady is expected to exhale her laughter.

I yelled for Kuka to come see and flicked on the switch. Dim yellow light flooded the bathroom and touched the blue tiles, honey-hueing the walls.

"Gosh!"

"Do you people see what I am seeing? This bathroom is exactly like the one in *The Bold and the Beautiful*," Kagonya whispered as she danced around the spacious bathroom, jiggling in her small, tight yellow dress.

I imagined myself lying in the bathtub, full of suds, just like the women in the Lady Gay TV commercials.

When Baaba asked if we liked the new house at the dinner table, a chorus of cheers erupted. Kuka joked that our old house's cement bathroom floor was as slippery as a snail. We laughed a little too hard. Even Mama.

*

Kagonya was not like the other maids. She did not drag me by the arm as I kicked. She did not use the rough kipanzi or soap my face with harsh imperial leather that stung my eyes. She didn't even force me to raise my foot so that she could scrub its instep as I held on to her dress. Instead, she let me soak in the tub until my hands became pale like a mzungu. All the while telling me stories. My favorite was the one about how Africans got black skin.

According to Kagonya Nyasaye, the monarch of the sky created the universe and all things seen and unseen. He took fresh clay and modeled for himself twin sons, Mwaafrika and Musuungu, to rule the world together. Nyasaye instructed them to go soak in the magic river. "The water's magic will make your skins." Mwaafrika, the curious child who loved to play, soaked in the water for a little while but was awed by the sun's majestic splendor and rushed out to feel its warmth. The clay on his skin hadn't soaked in the magic river for long enough, so it burned and burned and became obsidian black. This made Nyasaye angry. He thundered, "Because you have disobeyed me for the warmth of the sun, I shall send you to rule over a place where the sun is always hot." Mwaafrika's eyes sparkled as he turned to his father with a smile. "Nyasaye, I liked the warmth of the sun so much I was going to ask you to send me to a place where it always shines." Musuungu was too scared of his father to leave the magic river and stayed in the river so long that the magic water turned his skin white and thin, like a sheet of baking paper.

"Never forget this story, Kagai. Remember, yours is the skin of courage and adventure."

Kagonya's fingers would fold around the sponge as she squeezed suds onto the folds of my skin.

Sometimes, I playfully challenged her. "What about those women in Oloitoktok who use mkorogo to make their skin yellow-yellow. Do they do it for the men?"

Kagonya would slit her eyes and stare at me really hard. "See this child, poking her nose in adult matters."

"Just tell me; I swear, I won't tell a soul." I'd touch my index finger to the tip of my tongue and raise it to the heavens. Kagonya would follow my declaration with laughter so suddenly it sounded like a pile of luminarc dishes breaking on the kitchen floor.

*

The afternoon Mama found blue birth control pills in our bedroom, and the backyard was cooking hot. Kagonya and I were lying in the shade of the avocado tree, listening to Elvis Presley's croon on KBC's Midday Melodies. I turned off the radio when I heard Mama shout. Side by side, we rushed to the bedroom.

We found Mama bent over Kagonya's things, shaking the petticoats and dresses as packs of tiny blue pills fell to the floor. When I entered the bedroom, Mama put Baby in my arms.

She shook the pills in Kagonya's face. "What's the meaning of this? Who are you spreading your legs for, eh?'

"Give me those! I am 16 and independent." Kagonya lunged at Mama, but she raised the pills above her head so the girl couldn't reach them.

"You are stoking a fire that you cannot keep ablaze, Kagonya. You hear?"

Kagonya sulked for weeks afterward. I'd watch Mama say loudly to no one in particular, "A crooked sweet potato would rather be broken than straightened, but me, I will straighten the ones in my house at least." Kagonya would respond by muttering under her breath about teaching old women to mind their business.

*

Kagonya and Mama stopped washing together. They no longer laughed as they held the two ends of the soaking bed covers to wring out the water. The sulking Kagonya washed only after Mama left to buy omena and dried tilapia from Kibuye Market on Tuesdays. Mama's joy disappeared again, and I turned to Kagonya, who was like a sister, twisting my hair into bantu knots and teaching me silly songs.

Every Tuesday, Kagonya would place the radio on the bathroom sink, turn up the volume, and sing, mixing up lyrics and yelling out words in Lulogooli. Kuka at first called it a stupid mboch habit. He would leave in a huff to ride bikes around the Amalemba shops with his friends. That changed the day Kuka walked into the bathroom and saw Kagonya bent over the tub in a miniskirt. The trips to Amalemba stopped, and Kuka started coaxing Kagonya to share more of her tales.

Kagonya refused at first, shaking her head. "I don't want to brew trouble with old women." But she was sweet-talked by Kuka. Her name slid from his mouth so often that she finally gave in and smiled. She would tell us stories on the condition that a duty rota for washing utensils was drafted. I lent Kuka my Haco ruler and a red HB pencil, and he happily divided the house chores between the three of us.

We balked under the weight of buckets every Tuesday and watched Kagonya as she scoured the bathtub with Vim and sorted the clothes according to color. She'd block the tub drain, fill it with water from the taps, add Omo, then mix it until she was up to her elbow in suds. Only then did she start to tell us her stories. Kuka sat on an upturned bucket closest to Kagonya.

This went on for months, even after Kuka had gone to the hospital for circumcision and my maternal uncles came over to bring goats for his riaruka. Even after he started sagging his trousers and relaxing his hair with TCB Naturals Relaxer Regular, even after he started having wet dreams and writing letters to girls on the estate.

Mama and Baba didn't notice these things.

*

On the eve of Kuka's sixteenth birthday, Mama came home and found us sitting out on the verandah. We were roasting green maize and listening to John Karani's Groove Time Show on KBC English Service. Kuka was standing shirtless next to Kagonya, heating the metal teeth of the hot comb on the charcoal burner and passing it to her. I squinted in pain as Kagonya carefully passed the glowing comb through my hair.

Mama's voice floated to us from inside the house. She was calling me. I found her standing in the kitchen, holding a pair of scissors. Next thing I knew, she sharpened the teeth of the scissors *sha-sha-sha* on the kitchen cement steps and held me by the scruff of my neck, snipping tufts of my freshly straightened hair and leaving an uneven mango-shaped head.

"This will teach you something about listening to people's silly notions about beauty," Mama said. There was metal in her voice.

"Silly notions? Mama Kuka, if you don't want me to associate with your children, just say so. By hot combing Kagai's hair, did I hurt anybody?" Kagonya challenged.

Kagonya lifted her eyes to Mama's, and they stared at each other before she stormed off to our bedroom. Mama followed her and knocked on the door. Neither the spatter of frying chicken nor the clanking of teacups made her open it.

I wanted Kagonya to open the door. I tried to rub Vicks VapoRub on my sore neck and say, "Modi Kagai, sorry," but she did not. Later, I said to Mama, "Kuka relaxed his hair, and you didn't open your mouth; is it because he is a boy?" She only stared at me.

I am convinced that this was when Kagonya stopped caring about us.

*

When Kagonya opened the door the next day to remove dry clothes from the wireline, she had changed. We folded the shirts and dresses together and placed them in the clothes basket quietly. At dinner, the food tasted like cloth because Kagonya's laughter stayed stuck in her throat. She avoided our eyes and picked at her rice with the tines of her fork.

I didn't say a word to Mama when Kagonya and Kuka started listening to Salaam za Adhuhuri radio show on KBC Idhaa ya Taifa. I would press my ear to the closed door of Kuka's bedroom and listen to them argue about whether fans like Sura Mbili Kiango Momanyi, One and-a-Half-Lady and Kadenge Omwana wa Leah were genuine listeners or plants that regularly exchanged salaams to encourage other radio listeners to participate. I giggled whenever I heard Kuka promise to send greeting cards with Kagonya's name to the program. "I will make you a famous salaam queen by buying many cards from the post office and sending them to the show. I'll also ask MDJ Eddie Fondo to play you Peter Broggs's song 'How Much is That Doggie in The Window.'"

"Rrrrrrright!" Kagonya would respond, imitating Eddie Fondo's way of speaking. They would then dissolve into laughter, and I would swallow hard and listen as Kuka sang the song to her in his broken voice. Even before he finished the first part, Kagonya would laughingly interrupt him, and they would fall into an argument about its lyrics.

"It says the one with a beautiful tail."

"Nope, it says the one with a *girl-girly* tail."

"That's nonsense; how can girls have tails?"

"You tell me. You are the girl."

"I think boys are the ones with tails."

"Fine then. Consider me your doggie with a tail."

"And scare who away with one bark, eh?" Kagonya would giggle, and Kuka would bark like a dog.

They must have forgotten I existed. Even when he opened his bedroom door and found me there, Kuka would ignore me and rush to get his Pop Stop book with song lyrics cut out of the *Young Nation* newspaper. I wanted to stretch out my leg and trip him.

*

Mama's conversation with the estate gossip, Mukalishi, is what hardened my resolve to keep sneaking into the bathroom. Mukalishi visited us one evening, just after Mama had sent Kagonya to the posho mill to grind maize for ugali. I made them masala tea, and they sat on the verandah, sipping it.

"Mama Kuka, your house girl is illogically pretty," Mukalishi began.

"If you are telling me something, say it, Mukalishi."

"I'm not saying anything I don't want my mouth to say. But if I were the mother of a hot-blooded teenager who sags his trousers and shaves punk, a strong igirichi who was recently circumcised, I'd get a houseboy or stay home to mind my children myself."

"Not everyone has a rich husband, Mukalishi. If I stay home, what will they eat, *me*?"

"Fine, but ask yourself questions, Mama Kuka. Ask yourself why Kuka never joins his friends at the video stalls. Ask yourself what business he has holding pegs for a maid."

"Wallahi, if your words are true, I will skin somebody with my own hands," Mama replied.

*

The loud reggae tunes were soon replaced by smooth love ballads.

The sky on Tuesday after Mukalishi's visit was gray. Menacing clouds hung low and hovered as I sat in the garden, staring at bees dancing on the flowering purple sweet potato vines. I was annoyed because Kagonya hadn't sided with me when Kuka sent me away from the bathroom.

The book I was reading, *The Joker in the Pack* by James Hadley Chase, taught me a line, and I decided to sneak back into the house and peep at Kuka and Kagonya. If I found them doing dirty things, I would tell them what the beach boy's girlfriend said in the book I was reading: "Cold water helps."

I was surprised to see Mama back so early on a market day. I dodged her, rounding to the back of the house and jumping over the chicken coop to enter through the kitchen. As I pushed open the bathroom door, I beheld a sight so strange to my 12-year-old eyes that the nerves of my body twittered as if many isetwe birds were perched upon my spine. Kagonya stood inside the bathtub, tightly holding the handrail grab bar, back to the door. Her buttocks flexed like a closing fist as Kuka thrust into her over and over. Next to them, the golden swan faucet tipped its long neck and stared.

Kagonya didn't see me, for a terrible sound escaped her lips as she called out his name.

Mama chose that moment to walk in. Overcome with a spasm of grief, she gave a loud cry, "Kagonya, mkoláá kindiki, what are you doing?" Kagonya jumped away from Kuka, pulled up her orange panties, and made no reply.

Kuka calmly put on his jeans, walked past Mama, and got out of the bathroom. On the radio, Brandy crooned on, begging her lover to come a little bit closer.

Mama and I followed Kuka to the kitchen and watched as he poured himself a cold glass of water. Mama picked up the clay flower vase Baaba had bought while on a school tour of Ilesi pottery works and flung it at Kuka. It grazed his right hand, and the glass of water and vase splintered to the ground. Kuka ran out of the kitchen door, shirtless. I held my breath and pressed the laughter bubbling inside so that it wouldn't escape through my mouth.

Mama avoided my eyes. She locked the front and back doors, stuffed the keys in the pocket of her frock, and went to her bedroom. When she finally came out, she instructed me to wash the utensils and ordered Kagonya, lying on the bed in our bedroom, to cook the ugali. Mama then went to sit on the low stool, breastfeeding the baby and staring at the seveve, which was boiling in the sufuria, releasing its green. The radio sang faintly because the batteries were weak, and Kuka had forgotten to put them out in the sun.

When Kagonya came to get the mwiko, Mama, instead of handing it to her, slung it at her. It hit the girl's face. When she started screaming, Mama pushed Baby off, picked up the kiboko hidden behind the kitchen door, and beat the girl until her body was covered in welts the size of fruiting tamarind pods. Only then did Mama stop, and she ordered her in a choked voice to pack her bags.

Kuka did not come home that night. Mama stood in the sitting room, muttering to herself and shifting her weight from one foot to another. Kagonya, once ready, stretched her hand to Mama, who placed into it an old 500-shilling note.

"I won't have you underpaying me; give me the rest of my money." Kagonya's arms were folded across her chest.

"Get out. Have you not been paid in kind? Are you not the one who has taken my son's virginity?" Mama huffed, walking up and down the length of the room.

This amused me a great deal. I didn't know that boys could also be virgins.

A geyser of emotions shot up, filling the room. I tried to breathe.

"Five hundred, and you chase me out like a dog at this time of the night," Kagonya said. "Dááve, Mama Kuka, *no*. I'm not going anywhere unless you put all my money here." She beat her right palm into her left.

It was with a firm hand that Mama cast her out. I followed Kagonya outside. She removed her purple hairband and let her hair fall freely over her shoulders. She pressed the hairband into my palm and cupped my face in her hands. A stubborn half-smile lit up her eyes, and in the ensuing darkness, I couldn't see where her face ended or where her hair began.

*

The wild raspberries ripened and fell. My school blouse became tight around the chest. There were pimples standing on my once-smooth face. And Kagonya was gone. Gone was her laughter. Gone were her magical stories and silent movements through the house. She would have known what to do with my face, just as she had known how to quicken time and smooth the rough edges of our house.

Kuka was shipped off to St. Peter's Seminary Kamusinga to spend more time with the Lord and his fellow boys instead of in bathrooms with underage girls who wore short skirts that exposed flawless thighs.

New sounds started to fill my crispy December dawns. The whispery chatter of the milk boy I liked, the clanging of his metal pail outside my room, and the shrill voices of the vegetable vendors and their tauts of mboga, mboga. Still, each morning, as I watched the sun break its yellow yolk over the sky, I dulled at the thought of having woken up to yet another day without my friend, Kagonya.

Tsoro

Yes, get out of my way. Make room, part the Red sea. Of course, all heads turn to behold me as I enter the sprawling Mediterranean-style mansion, mesmerized, so predictable. Keep that stride, long confident steps, perfectly sculptured brown legs peeking as my turquoise skirt sways, my red-bottom pumps echoing the confidence of my stride with a steady, consistent tap on the hardwood floor. Let the glow of the sun that peaks through the large arched glass windows turn my skin golden, let my black hair shimmer in the brilliance, and watch as my eyes turn into a fiery orange-brown in the sun's glow. Chin up and look straight ahead, girl; they might cower if your eyes meet theirs. Save the cowering for later. They've never beheld such beauty, such force, such elegance, such command.

I set my purse, bright orange and shearling, on the dining table. Conversation and chatter cease. I give them a second to catch their breath and scan the room quickly—typical white men of varying ages in boring black suits. I notice two women in the corner, flat shoes, heads slightly bent facing the floor, stealing glances as though they need permission to be in the room. I clear my voice, puff my chest up, and speak loud enough for everyone to hear. "Good afternoon!"

Silence. Sigh—they need more recovery time. But I press on. "I'm Chiedza, your new Director of Infrastructure and Development."

I watch them shift their hands, unsure of where to place them. In their trouser pockets, folded on their chests, scratching their heads. They exchange looks, turning their heads to face each other, forming soft frowns, squinting as though the sun's rays are blinding them. An older man with a face woven in wrinkles, a sagging, loose skin, double chin, and white hair paces back and forth. In a dark blue suit with pink checkered lines, the young man next to him is clearly a rebel, deviating from the plain black of the rest, grins excitedly. I spot Peter, the founder and CEO of Solartronics, who interviewed me. He is six foot five and has dark brown hair that he clearly dyes as his gray roots are peaking. He steps forward and begins to clap. A crystal chandelier hangs above him. Behind him, the backyard is visible through the glass doors that lead to the patio. Beyond the fire pit, an Olympic-sized pool shimmers.

"Welcome to Wisconsin, Chiedza!" he announces as he approaches me.

One person claps. Peter waves his hands, encouraging the others to join in the clapping. Slowly, lazy applause erupts across the room. Chatter resumes as Peter shakes my hand.

"She's the diversity hire," The older man with a sagging double chin whispers to those around him.

"I don't care. She's hot. Can I be her intern?" the pink-checkered kid responds eagerly.

I turn to face them sternly. Let the cowering begin. They fold their personalities into themselves, avoiding my eyes, crocheting their fingers, and turning their bodies away from me. The young man is still facing me; I try to meet his eyes but realize he's staring at my hips.

"Welcome to my house," Peter says as he motions for me to follow him. "I'm glad you could join the offsite. Let me introduce you to a few people." As we walk past the bar, I glance at the wine selection the server in a white shirt and black bowtie has on the table and pass. For a man with a house this big, Peter sure does have poor taste in wine.

We meander across the house, through carved wooden doors, rooms with exposed beam ceilings, as he introduces me to everyone. Every time he makes sure to mention, "She's from Zimbabwe. Isn't that cool!"

He never mentions my Ph.D. in Physics, the ten years I spent running the semiconductor fab at Intel, my research on the degradation of organic solar cells that was published in the *American Journal of Physics* and the *Nano Energy Journal*, or the deals I've brokered for John Deere and Tesla, despite everyone's clearly questioning *"why her"* faces. I'm pretty sure he heard that diversity hire comment as well. I laugh to myself. I guess I'll have to get Peter in line as well. This will be fun!

"Where did Peter say she's from?" one of the two women in the room whispers behind me.

"I don't know, but she's some type of foreigner," the other responds.

Peter introduces me to the circle of people that has the old man and young kid last. I wonder if he thinks I should've forgotten the whispered words by now. "This is Chuck, VP of Engineering," Peter says as he gestures towards the old man.

I cuss internally, realizing the old man he is going to be my boss, he reports to Peter. Chuck chews loudly on his shrimp cocktail and nods, looking straight ahead at the aquarium.

"And this little guy is Jake. He's like a son. His dad and I go way back. We went to Stanford together, and I'm so proud that Jake is following in our footsteps. He'll be interning with us for the summer. I told his dad that Jake will always have a job at Solartronics," Peter says proudly before saying Greek letters in random order. Jake repeats them, and they both beat their chests twice with closed fists.

"So, what's your background?" Jake asks. I'm pleasantly surprised. He's the first to ask. I happily recite my decorated resume, highlighting my awards and dropping names where I see fit. From the corner of my eye, I can see the expression on Chuck's face change. He is clearly impressed. The others cower once more. That's right, bow down—I know my stuff, and I'm going to shake things up over here. Before you know it, I'm going to run this place.

"That's so impressive. I'd love to learn more from you. I just finished my freshman year with a 4.0, but I don't have a clear direction on what I want to specialize in. Peter, may I work with Chiedza for the summer?"

"Of course!" Peter says without hesitation.

Great, I get to babysit a frat boy! I'm going to have to find a way to lose him, quickly. Overload him with work, give him impossible deadlines, make him read research papers that are far too advanced for him, send him off to towns in the middle of nowhere, Wisconsin, to scout out new solar business partnerships with farmers—he'll be whining to Peter about how awful I am in no time, asking for a transfer. I smile at Jake and shake his hand firmly, squeezing it tightly and holding the crushing clasp for a few seconds to assert myself. He winces and I let go. Shaking his hand to get blood flow back, he takes a step back, sizes me from my shoes to my hair, then purses his lips as though he's about to whistle.

"Damn!" he says loudly. I smile.

"Lastly," Peter keeps going, "this is David. He's our Director of Quality. He's your counterpart, also reporting to Chuck

In his mid to late thirties, David looks to be about my age, and he's good-looking. I notice a ring on his finger.

"David has been here almost fifteen years. Started as an intern when the company only had thirty people. He told me then he wanted to run this company someday, and I knew instantly he had the grit and would do whatever it takes to be at the helm someday."

I stare at David's bland, black suit. He fits right in with the rest of the old crew. I will have to keep a close eye on this guy, but if his strategy is simply to blend in and maintain the status quo, I have nothing to worry about. David nods his head at me. I do the same.

Peter walks to the center of the room and stands next to the double magnum bottle of champagne to begin a toast. "What a rollercoaster this has been! After a scary year, we can finally press forward with hope and a winning spirit."

The crowd cheers and raises their glasses. I look at David, who is fidgeting with his ring. He recognizes the confusion on my face and leans over to explain as Peter carries on.

"Peter didn't tell you? We were about to declare bankruptcy, but Jake's dad stepped in and gave Peter fifty million dollars to pay off debt and invest in new technology. Peter is going crazy trying to change the company's image and reinvent us with the latest equipment, and...," he pauses and looks at me, "you know," he adds as he accepts a glass of wine from a server's tray.

"The little intern has been so annoying, walking around like it owns the place because of it's father's investment. Literally anything it suggests, Peter treats as gold. I guess he wants a good report back to Daddy after the summer. Good luck with that." David turns his head and joins the crowd in clapping and cheering at whatever Peter has just said as if he heard it.

I follow suit, but all I think about is the fact that I just sold my house in Miami and moved to Wausau, Wisconsin, and the president of the company I made these life changes for neglected to mention an impending bankruptcy. I exhale to calm myself, balling my hands into fists.

I try to focus on what Peter is saying. "To incentivize the employees, we are putting in place an aggressive tiered bonus structure. And at the end of the year, we will *all* vote for the employee who has contributed the most value to Solartronics—has led the pack in turning our business around. They will get a million dollars."

The crowd gasps. David drops his glass to the floor, spilling red wine on my shoes and sending tiny shards of glass across the floor. Peter laughs and raises his glass in our direction. "Yes," he continues, "whatever it takes, folks. Go big for Solartronics!"

The crowd continues to cheer. The servers ignore me as if they can't see the wine pooling at my feet. I make my way to the kitchen to find some paper towels. Alone amidst the stainless-steel appliances and an oversized island full of appetizers—bacon-wrapped shrimp, fried avocado, sliders, charcuterie boards with the widest cheese selection I've ever seen—I take a deep breath. A million dollars? A million dollars? Oh, you haven't seen the majesty of me. You have no idea what I'm capable of, what I can accomplish, the hardships I've had to bear, the depth of my resilience. That check is mine! I sit in silence for a few minutes, daydreaming about the possibilities.

"Oh, there you are!" Peter says, startling me from behind. I reach for the paper towel and wipe my shoes. "Are you ok? We got a server to clean up the glass," he says.

"Yeah, not to worry," I respond. David and Chuck follow Peter in the kitchen. I see the competitive yet desperate spirit rising within them. A childlike desire to be noticed, to be reassured, to become the favorite, engulfs their countenance. They follow him like puppies begging to be pet.

"Let me show you something," Peter says excitedly as he leads me to the fridge. A picture of a little black girl with a bald head and sad eyes rests on the counter, next to the fridge. "I sponsored a kid from Zimbabwe when I found out that's where you're from. The website had an interesting story about how tough her life is and what my money will do for her. Really reminds you about how lucky we have it out here," he says proudly.

I stare blankly at him, suppressing the urge to roll my eyes. Noticing that her name, Fadzai, is the same as my little sister's, I feign a smile and teach Peter how to pronounce the "dz" sound correctly. "Just like you pronounce my name." Much to his delight.

"Doesn't she have the cutest accent?" he says to Chuck. "I could listen to her speak all day!" He asks about my upbringing in Zimbabwe, and David, Jake, and Chuck listen in. I'm selective about what I share, focusing only on the triumphs along my journey, much to their disappointment. *A million dollars*, I remind myself—*you can stroke a few egos along the way.* "Well, Peter, this is great work you're doing," I say to shift the attention from my upbringing. "I bet you're changing this little girl's world."

Peter brightens. "Do you think we could do philanthropy over there? It could all be part of our rebranding? I want to make a difference in the world, find purpose, you know?"

I laugh to myself.

"Tell you what, why don't I lead this venture for you, for the company? Maybe we could plan a trip out there, couple it with some safaris or something," I offer.

Peter places his hands on his heart, his mouth hanging open in excitement.

"Let's not plan trips to Africa just yet," Chuck interjects, tapping his foot then clearing his throat. "There's work to be done and plenty of places in the US where we can go for team bonding escapades."

"Yeah, Peter, why don't we plan something in Aspen?" David offers. "We all know you love to ski. Three days on the slopes sounds amazing, doesn't it? Jake, didn't your dad offer his place out there if we meet our year-end numbers?"

Jake's eyes caress my body. "There's a hot tub out there. It's always great to wind down there after a day on the slopes."

"I love it! Let's do it!" Peter says. "I'll tell Hillary to clear all your calendars over Christmas," he continues as he scurries out of the kitchen in search of his admin.

My trip to Zimbabwe is already booked. Because I don't make it home often, my family tends to take time off work to be with me. And now I have to cancel? Peter didn't even ask if the timing works for me.

"I hope you ski," David says spitefully to me before he follows Peter.

Before I have a chance to recover, Chuck walks over to me.

"Listen," he says. "I'm a very simple man to work for. You'll either love me or hate me. There's no in-between. You do what I tell you, and we'll be just fine. Get with David and he'll tell you my expectations for checking in with me. A morning report of how you plan to spend your day, a mid-afternoon check-in so I can redirect, if need be, and an end-of-day summary. Don't ever suggest anything to Peter directly without passing it by me. So that little performance you just gave, not ok," he says with a raised voice, his face directly in front of mine, so close I can smell his shrimp breath. His wide shoulders hover over me. I freeze.

I'm a director! I will not be micromanaged like an intern. I will not allow my communication of ideas to the executive suite or board members to be edited, filtered, and possibly reclaimed with new ownership.

"Well, Chuck. I think we need to..." I begin but notice him lift his wrist and pretend to stare at his watch, intentionally communicating that he doesn't have time for whatever I have to say. I stop in disbelief.

"The baseball game is starting. Time to let loose. Business is done for the day. Pick your team carefully. This is Brewers' land," he says as he storms off. "Oh," he stops, turns back to me, and adds, "and I play a round of golf on Fridays, so don't disturb me tomorrow."

I hope he gets hit with a golf ball.

"He's right, you know," Jake says, startling me. "Lots of Brewers fans out here." I'd forgotten he was still in the room. "We start every Monday morning company meeting by discussing the game. They hate that I love the Giants, but I don't let them tell me what to do."

I don't know the first thing about baseball, but I'll learn so I can contribute to the conversation.

"Listen, do you want to grab dinner tomorrow?" he asks, leaning into me. "I can give you some insights about the company."

I want to squash this kid! I'm at least fifteen years older than he is. He's clearly the kind of kid who has always gotten whatever he wants. It's clear the fascination here, the one toy he's never had access to is a Zimbabwean one. I know I'm a creature that intrigues. Many a man have fallen in a single evening. But he doesn't know who he's dealing with. I will have him wrapped around my little finger. Some toys are dangerous, kid. You might lose a finger... or two.

"Let's join the group for the game," I say as I follow the cheers in the living room. I sit quietly, alone, in the back, watching my new coworkers react to balls being tossed, flung in the air, and uniformed men running around a field. There are a million dollars at stake. How do I solve this puzzle, ensure the money is mine?

When I was a little girl growing up in Mutare, Zimbabwe, we used to play a two-person mathematical strategy game called Tsoro. Each player dug ten holes in the ground and filled each hole with two seeds. The starting player selected which of their holes they wanted to play from first and dictated the direction the game would go, clockwise or anticlockwise, and that direction would have to be followed for the rest of the game. They move the seeds forward according to the rules and either gain more seeds or lose a turn. The game ended when one player had captured all the seeds in the holes. The winner kept all the seeds. I'd have to play my own game of Tsoro with each coworker. They'd all gotten a first-move advantage.

First, Chuck must go. I need to get him fired as soon as possible. I can't work for a prick. Jake is an easy pawn, and he's already taken a liking to me. I can use him to get Peter's ear. Make him sing my praises but loathe Chuck. If Jake says enough about Chuck's incompetency, he'll be gone. Better yet, what if Jake's dad said Chuck must go? David, I can keep, make it seem like I have competition. Besides, he doesn't seem to have a solid strategy. Peter's ego is so small, I can stroke it all over the place; it won't take long for him to favor me over David.

I took this job because I did research on how we could use existing dying Solartronic film technology to create new organic solar cells with increased efficiency, plus reduced or minimized degradation. I believe we can create a new type of cell that could have a far-reaching impact in providing supplemental energy and helping the planet go green. Farms could power bigger and heavier equipment and function fully off the grid. We could even incorporate these cells into clothes and use them to charge phones while running or to power tents for campers. Most of all, the cells would be cheaper than any existing material. If this works, Solartronic could become a billion-dollar company in a few years. I look over at Chuck and click my tongue in annoyance. But what do I know? I'm just the diversity hire.

"Chiedza, will you bake the cookies for Monday's celebration?" Peter says, interrupting my thoughts.

"You got it, Peter!" I respond.

I have no idea what they are celebrating. I also don't know the first thing about baking cookies. The room erupts in cheers as the ball flies across the field on an eighty-inch TV. I pull my phone out and google Jake's father. If he's driving funding for this company, I need to find out more about him. What's he into? What's his background? How can I leverage his connections and existing businesses to add value for him? What will it take to impress him? I'm delighted to find a plethora of information about him online. I could read up on him for days. I lean over and whisper in Jake's ear. "Just between you and I, can I meet your dad? I might be willing to grab that dinner tonight."

His eyes light up. "Yeah!" he responds enthusiastically.

I smile. Let the games begin.

Market Craze

No one cares that you're the best graduating student if your grad dress is trash. Last year, Fatima was roasted on 2go because she gave her valedictorian's speech in a wrinkled white jalabiya. That will not be me; I sold my laptop for a dress. The guy at computer village cheated me, but let's focus on the good part. The dress!! I had to find something that summed up six years of angst, tears, and tests.

On the Saturday before graduation, the Lagos sun came out in her glory and fury to enact vengeance on thousands of hawkers and buyers trudging the narrow street of Balogun Square. Balogun is a hot pot of efo riro soup. There is assorted meat, pomo, shaki, titus fish, snail, panla, and orishirishi vegetables, each fighting for air and space to survive. Sweaty bodies, traders, hustlers, humans, and spirits squished into me as I tried to navigate my way to the dress shops.

The woman next to me was moving fast for someone so burdened. She carried an infant on her back, a pot of ewa agoyin on her head, and an exhausted toddler tied to her wrapper. The infant on her back sucked a lollipop covered with catarrh dripping from its nose, creating a slimy symphony of slurping. That baby found something better than ecstasy. A complete contrast to the toddler holding onto his Spiderman shirt and mother's wrapper for dear life.

The pot on her head was the traditional metal gourd for party cooking except smaller. Red oil dripped down the pot's sides to her forearms. I closed my eyes and saw her trip. The steaming pot of mashed beans and sizzling palm oil splashed on everyone around her except me. The woman wearing a white jumpsuit next to her was covered in red oil and screamed from the burns. People shrieked and cried, blisters on their arms. Someone slammed into me, and I returned to reality.

"Sweet, Sweet Beans! Mama Ijebu Ewa." She shouted her wares at the top of her lungs, competing for customers' attention with every other sound in the market. The music shop blasted Pasuma from five speakers, the danfo drivers hailed passengers, "Ojuelegba! Ojuelegba! Surulere! Surulere!" and somehow, her voice sat calmly above the noise. "Sweet, Sweet Beans!! Buy Ewa Agoyin! Mama Ijebu Ewa."

The swish of her burdened back and the gait of her straightened figure did more to part the crowd than any motorcycle could. I followed right behind her, careful to stay far enough in case the pot fell but close enough to enjoy the path she was making in the crowd.

Two wheelbarrows collided into each other just ahead of us, creating a gridlock. The grain seller, whose millet was now soaked in the grime and puddle, rained curses on the yam seller, whose tubers were salvageable. The crowd tried to placate the traders and clear the road before the human traffic became unbearable. The traders would not budge and my anger exacerbated. I could be trying on designs and fabrics, but I was stuck in human traffic. The Beans Woman continued hawking in the standstill. "Sweet, Sweet Beans!! Buy Ewa Agoyin! Ijebu Beans for fresh Agege Bread."

I could not stop staring at her. She looked at me, and I turned away. The baby on her back was now rubbing his eyes and fussing.

She rocked him lightly, tipping over some oil to the irritation of the irate crowd.

I sighed and pictured myself walking down the hall on grad day in the most shimmery dress possible. The rustling beside me broke the trance. Beans Woman was searching her wrapper looking horrified; her toddler was no longer tied to it.

"Emma!! Emmanuel!! Emma! Where you dey?" the woman shouted. "Auntie! Auntie!! Which side he go?" she asked me.

I turned around in confusion. "Me? I don't know."

"Heiiiiiiiiiiiiiiiiiiiiiiiiiiiiaaaaiaaaa," she shouted.

Have you ever struck a peacock in the throat with a spear from a goldsmith's furnace? That's how she sounded. Her tears came in quick succession. The crowd thickened around us and the market grew louder. I could barely breathe. The grain trader moved the shouting and curses to gear 3. The Pasuma's voice and drum accompaniment reverberated through the market stalls. The traders, bus conductors, and rogues advertised their wares viciously. An Okada man revved his engine and plunged into the crowd. Commotion everywhere, I closed my ears to quell the panic in my chest. There was no opening through the mass of bodies.

The baby on her back started wailing. His nose dripped more mucus and the child kept sucking. Beans Woman looked at me like she was gonna lose her mind.

"Do you need help?" I asked.

She sized me up and took the pot off her head.

"Oh no no no no! That's too big for me to carry." *Who asked me to do this?* I screamed internally. She placed the pot on my head and miraculously slipped through the crowd, shouting her child's name.

My neck strained under the weight of the pot. I tried moving my purse to another hand, but I felt greedy eyes on me. I muttered a prayer that my dress money would make it safely to the boutique and tucked my purse into my bra. The plan was to help Beans Woman real quick and then find my dress.

I saw her wrapper in the distance and followed. The pot made it difficult to navigate through all the different bodies fighting for space. The warmth of the metal on my head rubbed against a balding spot on my scalp. Beans Woman kept shouting her son's name and running like a mad woman.

"Emma oo, Emma, Emma! Emma abeg! Abeg na," she cried, grabbing innocent people by the shirt to ask if they'd seen a small boy wearing a Spiderman shirt. I focused on following her without falling.

We reached a clearing in the marketplace, the timber section with thousands of harvested trees tied into bundles. There was no adult or child in sight, only old men sweeping wood shavings. Beans Woman knelt and banged her head on the ground. As I brought the pot down to get some relief, warm oil spilled on my clothes. I set the pot next to her and almost slipped away, but she started wailing.

"My pikin ooo! My pikin oooo! My child have loss. After nine months and two days labor, they have steal my child! My God!! I was selling market every day, till the time I born Emmanuel! My Emma oo!"

"I am sorry, ma."

"If na my market wey loss, I go fit bear am," she said. "This one na my child. You fit buy child for market?"

I had no answer.

"They have take my Emma. They have kill my baby. They have use my child to do ritual oo." She flailed her arms and legs in panic.

"Don't cry, madam. Your boy is safe. He may be laughing somewhere or even eating ice cream," I said, willing it to be true.

"Safe?" she laughed. "In this Balogun?" She pulled off her scarf and slapped both cheeks. The timber sellers stared at her and murmured. The baby threw away its sticky lollipop and started licking the mother's clothes.

Sunset loomed on the horizon, and I became paranoid. "We need to go, ma. Your baby is hungry. Emma can be on the way. Let's go."

I helped her up. She dusted herself and adjusted the wrapper holding the baby to her back. I pretended like I was going to carry the pot again.

"No ooo...give me." She pointed to the pot.

"Are you sure?"

"Don't worry," she said.

I hurried to help her place the pot on her head. As we maneuvered our height differences, the pot tipped, and its contents poured on the ground. The sand turned deep red as it soaked up the beans and oil. Her livelihood for the entire day was gone. Beans Woman started laughing hysterically. She laughed and laughed till her voice turned hoarse and cracked. I looked from her teary face to the spilled beans and then to the clothing stores ahead. Before I could say anything, one of the men from the timber stalls walked towards us.

"Madam! Which kind of nonsense is this one? You're messing our area nah," he said.

"My son have loss and you're shouting because my beans pour in your area," she scoffed at the man. She kicked her empty pot and walked away.

"Esan! My name," she said as we walked back to the main market.

"Esan, you *will* find your boy," I assured her.

"We *will* find my boy," she echoed.

We asked every person we saw if they'd seen a small boy about seven years old wearing a Spiderman shirt. The answer was no after no after no after no after no.

The market got darker, almost eerie, as shops started shutting down.

A black mannequin wearing a feathery, leathery, sequined gown caught my attention from the second floor of an outdoor boutique. I couldn't tell if it was a ball gown. It looked too extra. But that was the goal, right? To graduate from secondary school and shed this nerdy wallflower energy. Esan caught me looking at my watch and in the direction of the boutiques.

"By God's grace, I go find am," she said, "go buy your cloth."

"How did you know I was going to get a dress?"

"E dey your face."

"You will find your boy, right?" I asked.

She faked a smile.

The dress that determined my future was right ahead of me. I was on the second flight of stairs when I saw the police car parked on the other side of the street and a Spiderman logo screaming up at me through the car window. Alarm bells went off in my head.

"Emma! Madam! Madam Esan! Your boy," I shouted, jumping and waving my hands. Esan was in a far corner of the market, busy asking strangers about her son.

"Madam Esan!" I jumped higher so she would see me.

The little boy stared vacantly through the car's windows as I weighed my options. If I went down, I could get stuck in the crowd, howbeit dwindled. I had nothing to draw her attention with from up here. I looked down at my sandals and took a deep breath. What's the worst that could happen?

Ready. Aim. Throw.

The sandal went flying and kinda landed on Madam Esan's baby. The baby started squealing. She turned around and passersby pointed to the person who'd stoned her child with a sandal.

I waved frantically and pointed towards the police car.

"Your boy! Madam Esan!" I called out.

She looked confused.

"Emma! Emma! Emmanuel!" I shouted, continuing to point at the police car.

Madam Esan ran into the street without care for the cars or Okada drivers coming her way. Vehicles braked to avoid her and Okadas swerved to let her pass. She ran straight for the police car and started yanking at the door. A policeman dragged her away from the door and took her aside for questioning. I was too shocked to move, watching as they interrogated her.

The shop owner started taking the mannequins inside the store. The questioning continued. Madam Esan waved for me to come. The policeman pointed to his notepad and shouted something. Again, Madam Esan waved me over.

Did they need me to help prove the child belonged to her?

The shop owner called out to his neighbors to help him move more mannequins inside the store. Madam Esan waved me over. Emma punched the car window. Madam Esan held the door handle. The policeman pushed her away.

I ran up the stairs and didn't look back. The faint sound of wailing trailed behind me, but the cadence of my classmates' mockery drowned it out.

Her Name Shall Be Peace

The El Al Airlines plane from Tel Aviv touched down at Nairobi's Jomo Kenyatta International Airport right on schedule. Among the passengers in the elegant, blue-and-white Boeing 787-9 were thirty-six-year-old Ari Yaakov and his thirty-six-year-old wife, Zelda.

Mzee Lokol, a portly fifty-three-year-old Kenyan man in a t-shirt and loose-fitting trousers, was sitting in the arrivals lounge, reading a newspaper. There was a healthy number of people seated or milling around with baggage, but it was not overcrowded. Shortly, Ari and Zelda Yaakov entered the lounge, lugging wheeled suitcases. They were both wearing hats, but Lokol recognized them immediately.

"The Yaakovs?" he said, approaching them with a big smile. "Shalom!"

"Shalom!" Ari responded. "Mr. Lokola, I presume?"

"You presume correctly," said their genial host. "*Karibuni* Kenya!"

Ari had the lithe body of a tennis pro. His hair was black and wavy. He had a narrow face, premature crow's feet, and a long nose.

Zelda's long brown hair parted at the top, large eyes, clear skin, and a killer smile—such *a good-looking couple*, Lokol thought as he guided them through the airport. *But I probably weigh more than both of them combined!*

Lokol hailed a cab. The driver came abreast of the trio, opened the doors for them, and loaded the bags into the boot. Lokol sat at the front with the driver. Kiswahili rap music played softly from the music system as the cab left the airport for Nairobi City.

"Either of you been here before?" Lokol inquired.

"I have," Ari said. "Several times."

"First time in East Africa for me!" Zelda confessed. "I'm tagging along purely out of curiosity and a love for travel. I'm also hoping I will get inspired to shoot a film or take stunning photos."

"Film?" Lokol said.

"Yes, I'm a filmmaker," Zelda said. "Mostly documentaries."

'Oh, I thought you're also a water engineer like your mister!'

"Nah. I was an actress when we met at a harvest festival in our kibbutz. He kept staring at me. Eventually, he asked me for a dance."

"Yeah, when the wine hit!" Ari said, laughing.

Through the rear-view mirror, Lokol noticed the couple in the back seat interlock their fingers. "How big is your kibbutz?" he said.

"Two hundred families. Self-sufficient. We use drip irrigation to grow food in what would otherwise be a desert valley."

Lokol nodded sagely. "That's why you're here. We need something akin to kibbutzim in Turkana County."

Nairobi City. A bustling metropolis. Glistening skyscrapers, noisy *matatu* vehicles, horrendous traffic jams, weaving hawkers, and people from all walks of life crisscrossing the streets. Lokol took the Israelis to a restaurant overlooking Uhuru Park. They ordered local food and drinks and talked as they ate.

"Turkana County is in northwestern Kenya," Lokol said. "Vast arid and semi-arid land. Rubs shoulders with Uganda, South Sudan, and Ethiopia. It's many times the size of your home country, but there's very little development. The inhabitants are largely pastoralists, but they're in desperate need of drinking water for themselves and their animals. About eighty percent of people living in Turkana don't have access to reliable sources of water. Over the last couple of decades, we've had several drought seasons. Imagine how painful it is for a pastoralist to watch his livestock wither and die. Herders have been known to drive their animals into neighboring countries in search of water. Naturally, the water scarcity is also increasing conflicts as locals squabble over the blue gold. The government wants to find a permanent solution to the problem. That's why we're bringing in experts like yourself: to help us exploit the vast underground lakes in the region."

"I'll certainly do my best," Ari says. "What's the population?"

"About one million people, but scattered over a very large area."

"Are you a local chief or something?" Zelda pitched in.

"Well, I am an elder amongst my people, the Turkana," Lokol said. "But I'm here representing the government. I am your liaison, man."

"I see," Ari said. "Well, I'm sure solutions will be found once we get into the field and see what's available. In my company, we adhere to two principles: Work with what you have, and the solution is always in the environment."

After the African cuisine 'in town', the trio took an Uber taxi to Wilson Airport, near Nairobi National Park. Inside the park, wild animals grazed within sight of the city's skyscrapers. After about an hour of airport protocols, Lokola, Ari, and Zelda left Wilson Airport aboard a small Fokker 50-passenger jet. The destination was Lodwar, the headquarters of Turkana County. Ever the shutterbug, Zelda wisely picked a window seat. She happily clicked away at the vista outside, using a zoom lens camera, as the tiny aircraft sailed through the African sky. Far below, the landscape gradually changed from deep green to desert brown.

Even though the sun was beginning to dip, it was still daytime when the plane landed at Lodwar Airport, a small but surprisingly busy facility. Lokol guided his visitors to a waiting Land Rover with government plates and a driver inside.

"Your accommodation is taken care of," Lokol said as the visitors loaded their bags into the aging 4x4 vehicle. "You'll have a nice one-bedroom stone house not far from my place. You can even have supper with my family tonight, and wait till you see the view!"

"Oh, that sounds delightful!" Zelda said. "You're very resourceful."

They all got into the vehicle, which Ari noted was manual rather than automatic, and drove off in the opposite direction to the sinking orange sum. Unlike Nairobi, there were no skyscrapers, traffic jams, or crowds. Indeed, there were no roads to speak of, which made Ari realize why an off-road vehicle was the best option.

Once again, Zelda could not put her camera down. There was so much to capture.

"How cute is that?" she said, pointing to a herdsboy perched on an anthill, chewing on a twig.

The ground was sandy, occasionally dotted with green vegetation. Ebony-skinned people casually went about their business, some shepherding goats and camels. Children accompanied women and occasionally carried jerry cans or firewood. Zelda noticed that almost everyone they passed wore colorful jewelry—necklaces, bangles, anklets, earrings, and finger rings. His accessories were mostly beaded or metallic. There were no crowded areas—no estates, apartment buildings, or town squares. Occasionally, they'd pass small igloo-shaped houses made of flexible sticks.

"That's called an *ekol*," Lokol said, pointing at one of the conical stick-walled houses. "It's a 'day hut'. They're constructed by women. They also construct the animal pens."

A Turkana woman standing by the road in a long brown dress and numerous multi-colored necklaces watched the Land Rover as it drew near. She was carrying a shirtless baby who also had a fair share of ornaments on his body. The heads of both mother and child were shaved except for some spikes of hair at the top of their heads.

"What's with spiky hairstyles?" Zelda asked. "Do they signify something?"

"Oh, yes," Lokol said with the intellectual confidence of a college professor. "They're traditional hairstyles, and different clans may style their hair differently. It's an identifier. The little boy only has three islands of hair right now, but when he reaches warrior age, it will be more like a Mohawk. Girls usually grow their hair longer, though."

"Fascinating," Zelda said. "Can I take their picture?"

"We'll ask," Lokol said, and he asked the driver to stop next to that family. He then stuck his head out of the window and said, *Maata! Hawa wageni wanataka kuchukuwa picha zenu? Sawa?*"

The mother nodded. "She says it's okay," he said.

Zelda stuck her bust out of the window and took several shots.

"You see that silver ring around her neck?" Lokol said. "That's the equivalent of a wedding band."

Zelda finished taking pictures and drew her bust back into the vehicle like a tortoise, drawing its head back into its shell.

"*Ahsante!*" she said, waving at the family.

A short distance further, they arrived at their destination.

"We're here!" Lokol announced, pointing at a decent but unpretentious bungalow in the distance. "That's my place up ahead, and the house next to it is yours for the next few months." There were a few other houses in the general area, but no gates or picket fences. "And on the right is the county's most outstanding feature, Lake Turkana."

The visitors swiveled their heads and marveled at a majestic body of water shimmering in the dying light. A herd of camels was drinking water in the shallows.

"Wow," said Ari.

"That is *not* a lake!" Zelda said, gaping. "No lake is *that* big! I can't even see where it ends. That's an ocean!"

"Ha ha ha!" Lokol bellowed. "Behold the Jade Sea! The largest permanent desert lake in the world! Unfortunately, it doesn't have an outlet, so the water is alkaline."

The vehicle parked on the beach, leaving long tracks behind it like a desert snake. The passengers disembarked and retrieved their luggage.

"The Land Rover and its driver will be at your disposal," Lokol said as he led his guests to his house opposite the lake. "The Turkana National Water Purification Project facility, where you will be stationed, is quite some distance from here."

"Much obliged," Ari said.

Lokol led the Israelis up the steps to his house and opened the door.

"*Mama Watoto*," he said, entering. "We have guests!"

Presently, a dark-skinned woman with two missing lower teeth and the ubiquitous colorful jewelry appeared from the kitchen, followed by a teenage girl in a sundress and multiple earrings. Like her parents, the girl was so dark-skinned that her color matched that of her short hair.

"Meet my wife of twenty-five years," Lokol said proudly. "And my beautiful daughter, Akiru. Akiru is in college. Bright as a button."

When they had all greeted each other, Mrs. Lokol laid out supper. The main course was boiled goat's meat.

"My compliments to the chef," Ari said, sucking marrow from a bone. "Although it seems to me that you really consume a lot of meat, earlier today, Mrs. Lokol, your husband, took me to a restaurant where we ate beef stew, which he assured me was kosher and some *ah-gali*."

Akiru and her father burst out laughing.

"It's pronounced *oo-gali*!" the girl said.

"Oops!" Ari said. "I saw the name on the menu."

"That's alright," Mrs. Lokol said. "You'll learn a lot of things while you're here. And my husband *does* love his meat. How do you think he got *that* big?"

They all laughed in unison.

Zelda woke up at sunrise the next morning. She glanced sideways at Ari's sleeping form and then went to the kitchen to fix a breakfast that consisted almost entirely of fruits. It had been a hot night. The bed had only one blanket, and they promptly got rid of it. The air temperature was like that of a coastal or tropical island, and yet they were thousands of kilometers inland. Thankfully, there were no mosquitoes.

The lake outside fascinated her. She was a strong swimmer, and she craved to take a dip. After breakfast, she wore one of her husband's shirts over a brown bikini, put on a straw hat and Gucci sunglasses, and went out to the beach barefoot and alone. There were already a few people going about their business, including some young boys bathing in the shallows of the now-turquoise lake. She also noticed that all houses faced the east. She sat down in the sand, hugging her knees, staring at the waves of the world's largest alkaline lake. Before long, she detected movement behind her. Lokol and Ari were approaching.

"Is it safe to swim there?" she inquired of Lokol.

"Of course," Lokol said. "It's not even as saline as an ocean."

"They're no crocodiles or other creatures?"

"Not here. There's an island where crocodiles breed, but it's miles away. Very strong currents, though."

Zelda shed her clothes. She had a body like a seductress in a crime novel.

"You coming, sweetheart?" she said to Ari.

"Not now, honey," he said.

"Engineers!" Zelda mourned, rolling her eyes. "Always cautious."

"We have to be," Ari said. "If we make a mistake in the construction of a bridge or railway, people die."

Meanwhile, Zelda had already acquainted herself with the water. She was navigating through it with the ease of a mermaid, her long brown hair waving behind her like a superhero's cape.

Two days later, Lokol visited the newly commissioned Turkana National Water Purification Project (TNWPP) facility to check on progress. The plant itself was still under construction. The government was still looking for investment partners for their ambitious water project aimed at making clean water affordable and available to citizens *countrywide*. The infrastructure alone would cost billions of dollars and take decades to install.

Ari was in the water desalination lab, dressed in a white dust coat, when Lokol sauntered in with the confidence of a landlord. The lab looked like a pharmacy: labeled multi colored containers neatly arranged on multiple white shelves all around. There were various workstations topped with microscopes, Bunsen burners, and various chemical process setups.

"How goes the project, my good man?" Lokol said.

Ari wheeled around. "Not too well, I'm afraid," he said, shaking his head. He picked up a small bottle of what appeared to be water and held it aloft. "This is the tenth sample I have taken from the Lotikipi aquifer, our biggest prospect. It contains mineral levels that are seven times higher than the accepted global limit. It would take a lot of cleaning processes to make it drinkable. We may as well desalinate the lake. Which again would consume so much power that the water bills would be out of reach to the people we're trying to help."

"Damn!" Lokol said, bringing his fist down on a table so hard that the contents jumped. "I had so much hope in Lotikipi. That aquifer alone can provide enough water for the *entire country* for more than half a century! We need viable projects. Investors are waiting. Saudis. Americans. Bretton Woods Institutions. The problem is not getting the money. It's the viability of the projects. I'm tired of us being laughing stocks. Turkana has water and crude oil beneath its surface, but its people are starving. It's very hard to justify that to the world. We need a way to utilize our resources."

"Don't be too hard on yourself, old man,' Ari said calmly. 'Remember: the solution is always in the environment."

One day, a week into his Kenyan assignment, Ari got home, exhausted and frustrated from testing water samples, and flopped into a sofa made from reeds and softened by cushions.

"Babe, I'm home," he said weakly, in Yiddish, face down on the sofa as if he were waiting for a masseuse. "Babe?"

"You might have to find a Turkana name for me, sweetheart," Zelda's voice said from the bedroom.

"What are you talking about?"

"Are you ready?"

"For what?"

"For an African wife of Jewish extraction?"

Before his engineering mind could work out the calculations necessary to understand what his spouse was saying, Zelda emerged from the bedroom and struck a pose. She was dressed in traditional Turkana regalia! Leaf-shaped *akaparparat* earrings; metallic bracelets; a multi-colored and massive *ng'alaga* necklace; a large unclosed silver wedding ring around her neck; a beaded pinafore over the top of her dress; two strings of white waist beads; and decorated sandals.

"What do you think?" Zelda said.

"You look like a fashion model! Where did you get all that stuff?"

"I have been spending time with Mrs. Lokol. I mentioned how I admire how the land here is drab and dry, but the people are full of color. She told me I could get all the stuff I see women wearing. And that's not all. Since the Tokols are always inviting us to their place for meals and they eat so much meat, I decided to make them a brisket. Today, the driver and I went to Lodwar town, bought all the ingredients, bought all this cool stuff I'm wearing, and I made a brisket for our neighbors!"

"I thought I smelled something familiar. I thought I was just homesick or hallucinating from exhaustion."

"Besides," Zelda said. "They're always forcing us to eat their cuisine. Tonight, we give them a literal taste of our culture!"

Zelda wore the traditional garb at dinner that evening. Mzee Tokol tore into the brisket like a male lion, commandeering a carcass that a lioness delivered.

"If Nayece were here, Mrs. Yaakov," Tokol said between bites of the peppered kosher beef delight. "She would bless you and count you as one of her daughters."

"Who's Nayece?" Zelda said.

"The big heroine of Turkana culture, dearie," Mrs. Tokol said.

"Not just the Turkana," Mzee Tokol expounded. "The entire Ateker community, including the Jie of Uganda, We call her *Ataa Nayece*, which means *Grandmother Nayece*. This is to acknowledge her as the matriarch of our community. In actual fact, she was never married and probably had no biological children of her own."

"And yet she's the most revered member of the Ateker Community," Mrs. Tokol added. "She keeps us peaceful and united *to this day!*"

"That sounds fascinating," Zelda said. "You know I'm a filmmaker, right? I would love to hear more about your heroine. I love strong female characters. It's funny. A few weeks ago, I had never even *heard* about the Turkana people. Now, I'm in love with the community, and I just want to learn more! Can you tell me Nayece's story? Is it a true story or a myth?"

"Oh, she was *very* real," Tokol said. "We can take you to see her grave if you wish. It's a shrine that people visit even today. I can tell you the legend, but you have to remember that these stories were handed down orally, so there are some variations among the various communities. What I will tell you is the version that my mother told me when I was a boy. First, it's important to understand that the Jie and the Turkana migrated here from further up north. The Nile

Valley Basin. Probably somewhere in modern-day Sudan or Ethiopia. And they were definitely one person because they spoke the same 'Ateker" language. Our ancestors migrated southwards anywhere from five hundred to three hundred years ago. The Jie established themselves in Uganda and remained there to this day. However, probably due to population pressure or drought, a section of them—composed of mostly young individuals—traveled into this part of Kenya. They became famous for living in caves. They became known as the *Ng'iturkwana*—'cave people' or people from *aturkan*—'cave land'. The label stuck. And now we come to our heroine.

"Nayece was born in Jie Land, in Uganda. She later fled to Kenya, where she remained for the rest of her life. Some believe that the reason she fled was because her father, Orwokol, died, and some village elders tried to marry her off to a man known to be a domestic abuser. Deciding to escape her fate, she appealed to the spirit of her father, whom she revered. As she slept, she dreamt that her father appeared to hear her in spirit form and endorse her plan to escape, promising to guide and protect her. 'Your name shall be courage,' he said in a ghostly voice. True to the promise, Nayece arrived here—in Turkana County—and found a lush valley with a flowing river, luscious fruits, and wild berries. It was like finding an oasis in a desert. The backdrop was a hill now known as Moru a Nayece, or 'Nayece's mountain'. She built an *ekol* and settled down. She lived blissfully and peacefully in solitude, but as she aged, her chances of marriage and motherhood dwindled. She feared that the village elders back home had placed a curse on her. She consulted her father's spirit. 'My daughter,' the dream world apparition said. 'You called 'mother' by millions. They will look up to you for guidance and inspiration. 'Your name shall be peace.' 'Dad,' Nayece said. 'Last time, you told me it would be 'courage'. 'I did? Well, *now* I'm telling you that it will be 'peace'.

"One day, Nayece was in her *ekol*, cooking food, when two bulls appeared. One was black, while the other one was a rare shade of gray.

The bovine herbivores had probably strayed from a herd and become lost. The smoke from Nayece's house attracted them, knowing they'd find humans there. Since there was plenty of grass and water, the cattle remained in the area for days. Nayece neither domesticated them nor chased them away, figuring their owners might turn up one day. Sure enough, three warrior-like young men from Koramajong in Uganda soon arrived, armed with spears and shields. They found Nayece peacefully harvesting wild fruits. They were shocked when she spoke their language. They were fascinated by this fearless lone woman. Was she a witch? An oracle? A mad woman? Why did their cows go to her, and how come her area was so lush? They explained that the lost cattle were theirs. The gray one was especially sacred. Nayece agreed. She offered them her fruits and berries and allowed them to rest there. She told them her story, that she was an escapee from Jie land, the same area they came from.

"At night, the three men slept outside the *ekol* like sentries. They were used to sleeping under the starlight. A strange peace came over them. Why did the sacred cow lead them to this particular woman? Maybe the Jie were meant to migrate here—it was divine guidance. In the morning, they learnt more about the area. Nayece confirmed that it was indeed a very habitable area. Besides the Tarac River, seasonal streams occasionally formed. Green pastures being hard to find, the young men went home and returned with others to settle in the area, under the guidance of Nayece. She taught them survival skills such as how to start fires, cook food, and gather edible plants. In due time, some Turkana people also arrived, along with their livestock. Nayece was their natural leader. They believed she was a prophet and a seer. She divided the growing population into territorial sections that remain the basis of Turkana society.

"Before she died, Nayece issued an edict that all Ateker splinter groups should live peacefully with each other. She would also remain active in the spirit world for those who may seek her for blessings, guidance, and forgiveness. She had created a peaceful and happy community around Moru a Nayece, and she wished for it to be a shining example of inter-tribal harmony. When she joined the ancestors, her earthly remains were wrapped in a white cowhide, and her grave was covered with white stones.

"Even today, when conflicts break out amongst various clans or brands, the most surefire conflict-resolution mechanism is for the belligerents to perform a ritual around Nayece's grave. They circled the grave four times, confessing their misdeeds and asking for forgiveness."

Zelda was transfixed. She finally spoke:

"Oh my gosh!" she said softly. "That's such a powerful story. I want to film it and share it with the world. Will you be my consultant?"

"Depends," Tokol said, patting his enormous belly. "Will you bring me another lovely brisket tomorrow?"

Two weeks later, Zelda was sunbathing on the beach of the Jade Sea when she spotted Akiru, Lokol's daughter, being escorted home by a boy her age. The tall mahogany-colored boy was carrying the sticks common with herders. The youths were walking slowly, clearly enjoying some quality time. When they neared Lokol's gateless house, they hugged, and the boy went off in a hurry, presumably back to his herds.

"Akiru!" Zelda called out. "Over here!"

The dark-skinned girl walked over to the foreigner.

"*Maata*," she said.

"That means, 'hello'?" Zelda inquired.

"Yes," Akiru returned. "What do you say in your community?"

"We say, 'Shalom'. Actually, you can use it for 'hello' or 'goodbye'. It just means 'peace'... But listen. I have been thinking a lot about that documentary film I want to make about your heroine, Nayece. I want to cast actors to re-enact some of the scenes from the legend as a voice-over narrates the tale. Naturally, the most important role is that of Nayece herself. Would you be willing to play that role?"

"As in, I'll be in a film? Of course!"

"Great. My husband always says that one should work with what they have. So I want to work with your family. Your dad can play Nayece's father, and your mother can be the narrator. We're going to need at least three young men to play Nayece's discoverers."

"Erukudi can be one!"

"Who's Erukudi?"

Akiru jabbed a thumb over her shoulder. "That boy I was talking to just then."

"Oh!" Zelda said. "Is he your college mate?"

"He didn't make it to university. He's pretty depressed about it. He's back to being a herdsman. Actually, miss, do you think you can help him get a job at the water treatment facility? It's just that..."

"That what?"

"I don't know if I should tell you this."

"What do you have to lose? Dish the dirt."

"Well, he wants to marry me, and he can't do it without money or a proper job. Dad won't allow it."

"I see. The two of you are in love."

Akiru blushed. "We're childhood sweethearts. We've *always* been in love."

"Fine, then. I'll see if I can get him a job at the plant. I am sleeping with the chief engineer, after all. Ha ha... That was a joke. I'm referring to my husband. You're a virgin, aren't you? Sexual innuendo only makes you uncomfortable... *Anyhoo,* I think your boyfriend would make an excellent security guard. He already guards livestock all day. And there's new equipment being brought in from Nairobi for the plant. Security will have to be boosted."

"I can't thank you enough, Miss Zelda."

"Don't mention it. Now come, let me teach you how to make a good brisket. It might come in handy when you need to break the news of your engagement to your father."

Back at the Turkana National Water Purification Plant, Ari approached a seated Lokol with a sheaf of documents containing diagrams.

"What are these?" Lokol said, perusing them.

"'Ideas," Ari said, sitting down next to him in a white dustcoat. "Any large-scale water purification process will consume tons of energy. But in the course of my time here, I have become acutely aware of two things: the blazing sun and the vastness of the land. So, I commissioned two feasibility studies. One for solar power harvesting and the other for wind farms. The wind map in Turkana is amazing, and remember that the wind blows even at night. As for the sun, I'm surprised that the entire county is not solar-powered yet. Phones, homes, buildings, torches, and so on should be taking advantage of the endless summer. As for this facility, if we harness both solar power and wind energy, we can generate enough electricity to mitigate the energy bill from the national grid. Now, setting up wind turbines and solar farms is quite an investment, but this is for the future. It's sustainable. It will create jobs and help with the water project. We can't get anywhere near the total amount of clean water everyone in the county will need for themselves and their livestock, but half a loaf is better than no bread."

"Excellent," Tokol said. "I'll include these documents in my report for the higher-ups. I know that one day we'll find a permanent solution to our water problem. You know why I'm confident?"

"Why?"

"Because people like you are part of the Turkana community now. *And the solution is always in the environment.*"

They both laughed.

PART
TWO

She Lingers

I

Things became doleful after Adanne's demise. Her absence had a devastating effect on Ma, who would sometimes morph into a forgetful being. This is to say, Adanne's sudden demise became a malady that most days chopped away Ma's memory the way termites chop away the body of wood.

On such days, Ma would stare too long at the portrait of herself and Pa, long gone, that hung in the living room. The portrait depicted Ma in her wedding gown with a veil masking her face. She'd subdued her body into Pa's powerful arms. Pa, built like an edifice, didn't have much difficulty lifting his wife with his muscular arms, both peering lovingly into each other's eyes as if seeking lost treasures in them.

"Nwakaego," Ma called, her eyes still glued to the portrait. Not waiting for my response, she'd continue, "Isn't this enough trigger for a young woman to submit herself to a man?" She asked, pointing at the portrait as if I'd been oblivious to its presence in the living room.

"It is, Mama," I muttered, not sure where the question was heading.

"A woman is meant to be a flower, something tender and lovely, not a cactus that pricks men." She sighed heavily and let her shoulders droop in resignation.

Realizing where the conversation was heading, I kept quiet and let the ensuing silence envelop us.

"*Negodinu asanwam,*" she said, gazing at the portrait of Adanne while reveling in her beauty. In the portrait hung beside mine, Adanne was in her pinkish gown, letting out a peal of hearty laughter that furrowed her eyebrows and revealed the only two sets of milk teeth she had gotten on her one-year birthday.

"Don't you love how sweet your sister looks?" Her question came again. It was as if each portrait in the living room had a question attached to it.

"I do, Mama," came my response in a voice that lacked assurance.

"Who wouldn't? Your sister was such a goddess that would have fetched a good dowry for us," she said more to herself now than to me. "You see that gown..." I followed her hand to observe. "I bought it at an exorbitant price because I wanted to see my girl look pretty, and she did." She let out a smile that concealed her disappointment.

I thought of a way to distract her, to pull her out of this mental agony, but all my ideas seemed to have gone on a sabbatical at that time.

"But Ma, you can't continue like this," I only managed to say as I etched closer to relax my arm on her shoulder.

"You mean it's easy for a mother to kill the thought of a daughter who sucked her breasts?" She yanked her breasts angrily at me. I fixed my gaze in the opposite direction, looking again at Adanne's portrait, struggling to hide the tears that brimmed my eyes.

I felt betrayed by Adanne's death. More betrayed for the responsibility it'll saddle on me—constantly consoling Ma and trying to be her good daughter. I recalled the many fun memories I had with Adanne, especially the ones we'd played hide and seek as children. Adanne, being the oldest, often assumes the role of police, while I would be the thief she'll end up catching. Each memory was an open wound that became fresh and painful.

I'd curse Adanne for leaving us, especially Ma, who once told me how she had stillborns until Adanne came to stay.

II

Ma got married in her prime, when many mothers were encouraging their sons to bring her home, seeing her well-rounded waist as capable of producing babies. Many wooed her, but luck fell into Pa's hands.

Contrary to their expectations, the next two years of Ma's marriage didn't produce any fruit from the womb. They began to talk behind her back, some of their words falling into Ma's ears.

"Some of these pretty girls—you can't trust them." One had blurted out to her neighbor.

"She might have killed her babies with countless abortions. Forget her innocent face. These types are the real devils." The other added.

Ma had left the scene, bruised. She consulted her mother the following day. The woman, troubled by her daughter's plight, would lead her to several prayer houses for possible solutions. They'd pray, fast, and do all they were told, all to no avail.

As the days segued into weeks and weeks into months, Ma's predicament began to earn her the hatred and disapproval of her mother-in-law.

"Ezeobi," the woman had called her son one late evening, "should we start looking for another wife on your behalf?" Her question was more like an instruction to a ten-year-old child to do the right thing.

"Don't. Mama, where's your faith?" Pa had asked with a face wrinkled with worries. He, too, was troubled.

"You don't talk of faith with a lady who has sold her womb. Ezeobi, I gave birth to you when my breasts were still standing firm like an erection." She'd paused to inspect her son's countenance. Ma, who had been eavesdropping, sobbed silently from her corner. She knew a day like this would come.

"Tell me, when will this he-woman conceive? When her breasts are flattened like deflated balloons? When she reaches menopause, eh? *Gwa m*," she groaned. "I want to carry my grandchildren before joining my ancestors. *Inugo*?" She resumed, cupping her palms as if carrying an imaginary baby.

"I've heard Mama. You will," Pa replied half-heartedly.

Ma's pregnancy the following year was greeted with surprise. Her mother-in-law luxuriated in the euphoria that came with it. But when it turned out to be stillborn, her worry resurfaced. Ma had four other stillborns and finally resigned to fate.

"It was *Ndi Iro* who must have done this," she resorted to blaming her enemies for her bad luck whenever someone expressed sympathy. She'd later encourage Pa to find another wife.

"*Dim*, my husband, Let's get a fecund woman to give you what my *chi* has denied me." She'd told Pa, who let out a sad laugh before declining. Ma felt pride and shame at the same time. Pride for knowing her husband didn't build the marriage on the bedrock of child-bearing. Shame for her inability to bear a living child and quell the mouths of men.

It was of no surprise, then, why her faith waxed stronger in the God she met at a local church, where the pastor assured her that she would carry a living child just months before Adanne's birth.

She'd watch, with skepticism, Adanne's maturation from a toddler that troubled the floor with the pitter-patter of her feet into a healthy one-year-old baby.

There was now the trouble of having another child. Worries sneaked back into Ma's heart. She knew one was not enough, especially a girl who wouldn't give her footing in Pa's home.

She gradually began to pour all her love on Adanne, over-pampering the girl, responding to her every childish antic, and shivering at any little thing that happened to her.

"Mama. Mama, I've hurt myself." Adanne came crying one evening after inadvertently hitting her toe on the whetstone outside the compound.

"*Gini?* Oh Lord, please not this time," she rushed out from the kraal, where she'd been supplying fodder for the goats. "Come and show me." Ma's heart was already pulsating with fear. Adanne limped towards her, still sobbing.

"*Ndo,*" she said, inspecting the wound. "Sit here and wait for me," she said, directing her to a chair. Adanne sat while Ma rushed to boil water in the kitchen.

She'd return a moment later to dab the wound with hot water. Adanne cried as the water seared the flesh in her toe, where blood had begun to congeal.

When Nwakaego finally came eight years later, Ma's worries shriveled. She became a bit more relaxed, though disappointed at not having a boy.

"At least no one will open their mouth and call me barren again," she'd once told Pa ecstatically. "Though a son would have been an added advantage."

"You worry too much, this woman. Haba! Must you always question your *chi*?" Pa thundered, too content to be piqued by his children's gender.

In the following years, when no other child came, advice began to fly like locusts into Pa's ears.

"Find another wife, Ezeobi. These girls will not inherit your wealth, *mancha;* they will marry and leave your home." The men had sounded their warnings like a gong, pulling their ears to punctuate each word that fell from their mouths with emphasis.

Pa had padded his ears against their advice; hence, he didn't flinch a bit. Their marriage became more peaceful with each passing year, except for Adanne, who was gradually growing into a thorn that pricked the hearts of her parents.

"*Okwa*, I said that this child would be the end of me. *Legodi*," Ma would lament, pointing scornfully at Adanne's masculine gaits. "See how a daughter from my womb wants to tarnish my image." Ma would burst into tears, wondering what had come over her fast-growing daughter.

Seeing me as being tamer than Adanne, she took succor in me. Our home, most nights, has become either a church or school, depending on who was in charge.

"Adam," Pa, who was more mild with Adanne, had called her one night. He was always cooler when educating his ignorant student than Ma, whose words to Adanne were often fire and brimstone, daring to cut her open and remove the demons in her body. "Don't you think you'll be more lovely when you behave like the person your *chi* has created you to be?" Pa asked. He continued to give Adanne a series of lectures on reasons she should keep her head, which Ma said harbored demons, calm.

Adanne had acquiesced to his advice. She willingly comported herself, especially whenever Pa was around. The years have seen them become inseparable.

It was no surprise that she broke down when Pa died of lung cancer. Adanne was eighteen then. Disappointed at the death of the only man who seemed to understand her, she began to retreat into her shell. She avoided both me and Ma, whom she distanced herself from as if she had suddenly become a plague.

Ma became frustrated by the turn of things—Pa's death and Adanne's behavior.

"Adanne, do you ever pity your mother at all?" Ma had managed to ask one day when she could no longer bear Adanne's distancing and boyishness

"*Nwam*, you know you're beautiful? You're the kind of woman every man would like to marry and flaunt around." Ma peered into

Adanne's unflinching eyes to see if her words were creating any effect. "Look at me; see how wretched I am." She stood to let both girls inspect her body, which had begun to lose its robustness.

"Do you want your mother to continue suffering like this? You're of age, my daughter; find a husband who'll remove reproach from our home," she implored.

"Okay, mama," was Adanne's only response. It lacked assurance, but Ma found it more conciliatory than a blunt refusal.

III

It was of little wonder then why Ma's disappointment grew wings when Adanne, at twenty-eight, chose to remain single. Her boyishness made Ma believe that her enemies changed the gender of the male child her *chi* had wanted to gift her.

There was something perky about Adanne—her gregariousness and conviviality, which attracted friends to her. The only thing eccentric about her was her strong preference for male things, reflected in her choice of clothing, coupled with her athletic looks and masculine gait, which scared some men from approaching her.

Adanne never wore any clothing meant for ladies; she preferred those of her male counterparts—baggy trousers, oversized shirts, denim jackets, hoodies, and suits. You couldn't enter her room without mistaking it for a boy's. But Ma had banned me from entering her room; she feared I would contract the disease from regularly visiting a room that she believed had been inhabited by demons. Too overwhelmed with grief, I'd always find a way to sneak in without attracting Ma's attention.

She once lured Adanne to the house of our pastor to undergo some exorcism. It was on a Sunday evening. Adanne loathed the church and the people it harbored. She had blatantly admitted this on countless occasions, condemning the worshippers of the religion that treats her like a pariah when Jesus implored everyone to come to him as they are.

After being welcomed, we sat at the pastor's upholstered chairs, with me close to Ma and Adanne, and in the opposite direction, close to the television.

"My daughter has been possessed, pastor. Please pray for her," Ma's words rolled out of her mouth, her voice quivering.

Adanne frowned at this pronouncement, cast an angry look at Ma, and managed to restrain herself.

"*Ogini*, what is it?" the pastor asked, though aware of Adanne's behavior. Once, at the pulpit, he condemned the likes of Adanne, whom he said posed questions to God over his work of creating man.

"See her there, pastor. Let her confess her sins and ask God for forgiveness," Ma continued, muffling sobs as she recoiled like a prodded worm at the utterance.

I stole a look at Adanne, only for our eyes to meet. I saw hatred boldly written on them.

"*Bia,* Mama," she called while springing to her feet. "Must you always disgrace me like this?" She asked, seething with anger.

"Sit!" The pastor thundered. Adanne, rather than comply, hissed and made for the exit, leaving the pastor's mouth wide agape in disbelief. She muttered words none of us could pick. Speechless, we followed the receding figure of her back until the distance swallowed her.

"You've seen your sister? She has sworn not to let me drink water." She puckered her lips at the utterance, clasping her breasts as if she'd suddenly gotten cold. I fought for the right words to reply to her, but none came. Words often desert me on days like this, so I waited for the pastor to speak. The visit created a rift between Ma and Adanne.

Adanne's intransigence bore children with each passing day. One evening, she came home with two girls, whom she bluntly introduced as lovers to us.

"Good evening," the first girl, with skin the color of burnt milk, muttered to Ma, who didn't respond. The other, sinewy like cassava stick, didn't greet. She kept chewing her gum the way a goat chews its cud, pausing and resuming at intervals.

"Adanne, can't you at least respect Ma a little?" I asked after leading her out of earshot.

"Is that what she instructed you to tell me? Okay, fine. Kindly go and ask her if she respects me and my decisions." She retorted, returning to where she had left the girls. Again, my effort to unite these two had proven abortive.

"You're heartless!" I let out, not minding whose ear the words would fall into. As if stabbed, she paused, fired me an angry look that left my face drooping in regret, and instantly made for her room with the girls, bolted her door, and left us wondering what might be going on between them.

In the next few minutes, they broke into sensual laughter that culminated in moans. Ma instantly dragged me inside the room, where she'd stifled my ears with her fingers against such an ungodly sound. She saw it as an epidemic that could easily infect me.

"Stay here, *inugo*? If you don't know what to do, carry your Bible and read." She instructed me, amused me, and angrily made for Adanne's door.

"Who are those goats that wouldn't let me hear a word?" She asked, banging at the door.

"Open this door before I raise an alarm," she threatened as she exerted energy to force the wooden frame open. Silence ensued between the girls. Ma kept knocking and banging intermittently at the door.

"Adanne, stop desecrating my house before God punishes you." her voice was laden with sorrow. She gave the door a last push that saw her wrapper getting loose. She stopped in time to tie it firmly before resuming.

"Mama, you can't continue like this. Please, take it easy, Abeg." I consoled her, leading Ma into the room as she kept mumbling angry words. The girls sneaked out of Adanne's room, careful not to let their footsteps attract Ma's attention. But Ma had noticed them but chose to feign ignorance.

Every night, Ma, who shared the same room with me, would ensure we clogged God's ears with prayers before laying our tired limbs on the springy bed to rest.

Adanne, who had a separate room, had exempted herself from the ritual.

"Why should I join you both in that prayer session?" She had asked me the first time I implored her to join us.

"So that she'll start one of those sermons that condemn me to hell before the coming of Christ?" She'd asked sarcastically. "I know you think well of me, but for prayers, forget it," Adanne said with a mark of finality in her voice. Her mind was made up. That was the last time I tried persuading her to join us.

This night, Ma and I had begun our prayers again. Ma took the lead; her pleas accentuated in Igbo.

"Father, Lord," she started, clasping her hands. "*Biko zoputa nwam,* please save my daughter," she would plead, her whispers battling not to escape the roof of the building, for fear of having *Ndi Iro* catch her words and use them against her. She would fold me like a mattress into her bosom before imploring me not to follow the ways of Adanne. I would nod in compliance, afraid that any sign of mulishness from me would make Ma suffer a heart attack.

The first time Ma developed a heart attack, Adanne had come home with her male friends to smoke *shisha* in the confines of her room.

"Please leave my house," Ma had ordered Adanne's friends, her hands pointing at the exit.

"Guys, relax. Make una chill," Adanne told them. They'd paused as if contemplating what to do next.

For the next few minutes, Ma and Adanne stood staring at each other, silence building a bridge between them.

"Mama," Adanne started, "why must you always stand in my way?" She asked.

I etched closer to them, confused about whom to confront first. Not wanting to offend any of them, I went subtle.

"Adanne, you can always smoke outside. Live part of your life away from Ma's presence, at least."

"What nonsense life is she even living? Look, Nwakaego; has she infected you too? *Heu Chimo*," Ma let out a wail, clasping her head with both hands.

Adanne hissed, raised her middle finger at me, and returned to her hookah. The smoke from the hookah tangled in circular motions and traversed her room before wafting into our nostrils.

The smoke, or rather, the pain of having such smoke emanate from the ungodly act of her precious daughter, made Ma cough hard, pucker her face, and curse Adanne with bated breath.

"May it not be well with you. You want to kill me before my time, *okwaya*?" She had asked sardonically, clasping her chest before slumping on the floor.

"Please, you guys should go," Adanne instructed her friends, who, stunned by Ma's sudden collapse, had rushed to help her up only to be restrained by Adanne. "I say go!" She shouted. In compliance, they sashayed out of the scene.

"You've seen what you've caused now, right? I hope you're now satisfied." I asked with a voice tinged with both fear and worry.

"Hey, hey, this is no time to cast blame." Adanne had frantically removed her starched long sleeves, using them to fan Ma before lifting her effortlessly with her hands, which had become muscular like those of a heavyweight champion. I watched tears trickle down her hazel eyes for the first time in ages, her mouth muttering words that sounded like a prayer, for I heard the name of God in it and wondered if God would hear too if he wouldn't close his ears the way Ma closed mine whenever those girls moaned in Adanne's room.

IV

Ma's curse killed Adanne. I know this from the way it followed her like an ant sniffing honey. She died just a few months after the curse.

The day death took Adanne, she was in her red Moroccan men's caftan. She held a fellow girl like a tulip, walking hand in hand with her, their faces coated in happiness, down the boulevard. She'd paused across the boulevard and plastered the girl's caramel-colored cheeks with kisses, not minding the glaring eyes. I was at one corner of the street observing them, fear tucked neatly in my heart like the uniform of a school child.

I walked in their direction, desperate to part both. The carefree attitude of the girlfriend, who leaned her weaved head on Adanne's shoulder, angered me.

"*Tufiakwa*—God forbid," I heard one of the onlookers lament. He spat out saliva and whirled his hands over his head before snapping his stubby fingers.

"Aru!" an elderly woman exclaimed, seeing Adanne's action as an abomination, for it's abnormal for a girl to confess loving a fellow girl in my place.

"Does this girl have a scrotum between her thighs?" the third, a businessman whose son has been pestering me, asked sarcastically, making the rest burst into laughter that was soon swallowed with frantic demand for fuel and matchsticks. My courage slumped. I stood transfixed in my corner, contemplating what to do.

I briskly went toward them. "Adanne," I called, my voice too tiny to reach her ears. I heard the sound of rolling tires. Adanne looked in time to meet my gaze and the young men coming toward them.

"Run!" I shouted, willing my voice to transport her away from the scene.

Just then, a tire haloed her head like a necklace, aborting her first attempt to flee. The young men circled her. I watched the girlfriend slip away like a fish, and a lump of anger seized my heart at her betrayal. She'd brought Adanne out in the open just to expose her anus. I charged in, willing to be burned with Adanne.

"Nwaka go. Ma needs you now more than ever!" She shouted with a pulsating heart. I felt strong arms bundle me out like firewood. Tears had blurred my eyes from viewing whose arms those were. I kicked, panted, and struggled to be freed from them.

My ears caught the explosion from where they'd confined me. They'd set her ablaze. She burned. They burned her. They said they'd caught her in the act. I watched her ashes fly up towards heaven as if running to table her complaints before God. Her bloodshot eyeballs stared hard at me as if scolding me for an unnamed crime. I freed myself and ran to hug her ashes.

"This girl is going crazy," one woman shouted. I didn't mind.

"What do you expect? It was her blood that got burned," another added in a consolatory tone, though the pity was mostly for me rather than the dead Adanne.

I took the ashes home to stay closer to her after her death. I gathered them in a bottle, which I hid beneath my bed, from where I would fish them out every night before I went to sleep, to offer prayers to God on her behalf.

"Dear God," I would begin with a voice heavy with sorrow, "please let Adanne find fulfillment in paradise. Don't let her experience a second hellfire." I would continue till the night drowned out my voice.

V

Ma was a loner. She started turning inward for comfort after Adanne's death. She avoided everyone and took solace in her own company. Sometimes, I would find her in Adanne's room, where she would gather Adanne's things and commune with them as if they were her daughter.

"They killed you because they thought you'd spoil their chances of having potential inlaws, *ndi ara*," she would say, hugging the clothes and crying her heart out.

Adanne lingered. Ma still banned me from smelling her room. She thought Adanne still inhabited the place and would initiate me at my entrance. Too overwhelmed with grief, I'd find means to sneak in without her notice.

"Adanne," Ma would call me, mistaking me for my dead sister. "When will you get married and let me come for omugwo?" She would ask, as if coming for postpartum care was all that there was to her now livid existence.

"Very soon, Mama," I blurted out, unsure if I meant the assertion or was only trying to placate her worries.

"You remember Chika? Dee Okonkwo's last daughter?" She asked. I nodded.

"She's tying the knot." Silence followed her words as I glimpsed a chicken joyfully pecking leftover rice. "I heard her husband is based in Lagos."

"That's great," I muttered, not sure of what else to say.

"Nwakaego," she called, as if suddenly realising her mistake of transferring Adanne's name to me. "Please, don't be like your sister; accept one of these good men, and settle down, *inugo*?" Her voice implored. I saw the frustration on her face.

Fear began to consume my body. It came most days like a spasm, taking over my emotions and causing my heart to thud at the memory of my sister. Each memory was an open wound that oozed sorrow. I began to see her in my dreams. I wondered if it was just a figment of my imagination, as I would often wake the following day feeling empty and dejected.

"Nwakaego," Ma's shrill voice broke through the compound as I made to set off for a program.

"Mama," I responded, gliding back in her direction, my steps oozing confidence.

"Go well," she smiled with pride written all over her face. Proud that I've grown to become the exact opposite of Adanne—being seen more in women's wear and maintaining feminine strides, which Ma believed would make me a cynosure in men's eyes.

VI

This morning, I ran my hands over my afro-hair, now tangled by the Harmattan that began a few days ago. Gently, I divided them into sections, oiled them, and combed them back to normalcy.

I ransacked my makeup bag and brought out a concealer, which I applied to my acne-dotted face. I decked my wide lips, which a friend once teased were overly wide from too much crying, with a burgundy lip gloss, making them look lovelier. Not wanting to cheat on any part of my face, I penciled my eyebrows till they assumed the shape of a willow leaf. Satisfied, I stood and swirled a little to inspect my red flowing gown with feather embroidery—I must look cultured and genteel before Chinua, who just came back from America.

Chinua and I first met in college, where he confessed to loving me before going abroad. Last week, he called to inform me that he was back and invited me over. My heart thudded so much that I feared he must have heard the sound and calculated the number of butterflies that swarmed in my belly.

A gentle knock on the door distracted my attention. I paused, fixed my gaze on the door, the key dangling at its knob, and told whoever was there to come in.

It was Ma, with hands akimbo—smiles littering her face.

"Nwakaego," she called without mistaking me for Adanne; she clutched her smile like a jealous lover. The smile was familiar to me; it was the kind she gave whenever she was in a gay mood.

"You've been a great consolation to me. You made this grief appear light like a feather." She confessed.

"Soon, you'll come for *omugwo*," I assured her. She ran to me at this utterance and folded me like a mattress in her arms that had become too frail and worn out from age and grief.

"I know you wouldn't fail me. God bless you, *nwam!*" She'd raised her voice at the last utterance as if afraid that failure to do so would stop me from being her daughter.

I peered into her eyes and saw the image of Adanne. Suddenly, I felt abandoned. I discovered how hard it would be for me to stop missing my sister. Something told me she would find her way back to my life again. Maybe come as a good son who'd find happiness in my home.

I wanted to tell Ma that Adanne would come back as she'd wanted to be. I decided against saying it, afraid of resuscitating a painful memory and because our religion doesn't believe in reincarnation.

Ma felt frail and sweaty, but she held me like she would never let me go. At that moment, I felt fulfilled for managing to fill the vacuum left in her life by Adanne's demise, even though it left me emptier. I've gradually come to accept the responsibilities Adanne's death saddled on me. I kept clogging God's ears with her name, till I believed that God, tired of my disturbance, must have dragged her to her bosom, where no one would come for her.

Half Portraits Underwater

In the school's auditorium, my sister, Yagazie, is still dancing. She moves like a masquerade in a trance. Her fingers twirl, her hips sway, her body pirouettes, and the beads around her waist slither along with her. Afrobeats her guiding wave.

This is how I see her now that she is no longer with me.

I sit in the middle: ninth row, fifth chair. I retrieve my book. When she dances, I write, and her body speaks poetry. Dusk invades. No one else is around. She likes it this way: the interplay of sound, silence, and her body movements. She contorts her shoulders. The tempo rises, and as she turns with the rhythm, the late school bus purrs to life. I call out her name, but the music shatters my words. I rise to tell her. Sweat drips, and her smell of pepper encircles me as the music reaches its crescendo. I reach out to her. She fades, merges with the air, and I fall on where she danced.

***

"Olioma! Olioma! What you dey do? The bus na wan leave," a girl says behind me, rushing out before I see her.

I sit at the front of the school bus. Behind me, at the back, the girls who play hockey laugh. Yagazie and I used to sit with them. I didn't talk to them much; each time, Yagazie was my avatar in conversations. Once, they tried to get her to join the hockey team, but she loved dancing too much.

The bus moves through the traffic. Ikoyi has a quiet, dilapidated charm; today, it feels like a grandfather with long white hair, while Victoria Island sounds like Papa's baritone, deep and reassuring. We live in 1004 Estate. I alighted at the street near our estate gate. The street sleeps through the day and rises at dusk. A heavy-set woman serves jollof rice to okada men. Further along, fruit sellers have set up stalls; they sell pineapples, bananas, watermelons, and mangoes. They don't sell plantains, which I like; they're sold on a different street, a small distance from here, next to the Chinese restaurant. Yagazie always bought me some, even when I didn't want any: she stole money from Papa when he refused to buy something for us.

Trees rustle. The air smells of mint and loneliness. Cars move slowly past me and into the parking lot—so slowly, you wouldn't believe it's Lagos. The apartments are lit up in patterns I know well. The Yoruba woman's lights are on: she exports Ankara suits to a store in London and stays there for the first half of the year. There's the politician's apartment: he brings his mistress every second Friday. Then there's the Swiss expatriate who is home every day by six; once, he complained to Yagazie about the rudeness of Lagos drivers, but Yagazie told him it was his fault he had left such an orderly country to come and live in Nigeria.

As I enter the lift, the gateman greets me: "Good evening, Ma." He calls me "Ma" nowadays. Five years ago, he used to call Yagazie and me by our first names. When we grew breasts (Yagazie first), he changed. Yagazie liked being called "Ma." She preferred to think of herself as mature as Mama. I don't like it at all; it makes me feel older than I am.

Our duplex is on the top floor. We used to be the four of us—Mama, Papa, Yagazie, and me. Now it's just me and Papa. We have a housekeeper, Taiwo. She comes in the morning and leaves when I come back from school. I open the door to find her waiting for me. She's holding her bag, ready to leave. Her phone rings, but she ignores it.

"Aren't you going to answer?"

"No, Ma. That's my broda. He is useless." She points to the kitchen counter. "Your food is there."

"Your twin brother?"

"Yes. He wan chop life with no wok. Every time, he asks me for small-small moni, and he's doing nothing in Ibadan." Her words float out with her. She waves goodbye and closes the door.

Every crevice in the house is colored by Yagazie, especially a photograph of Mama, Papa, and me at her requiem mass. Mama said her spirit moves through the house sometimes, urging Mama to run after it. Mama said she noticed it when the harmattan began. I saw it, too, but I lied when Papa said he hadn't seen anything. And so Mama moved to Enugu to stay with our grandmother and aunties. She has been away for months. I couldn't imagine her leaving Lagos; Mama loved the city, and she loved her job as an interior designer. Lagos has been a part of her ever since she found work here in the time of Abacha.

Nowadays, the grief Mama carries burns everything she touches. Yagazie was her favorite child. She was the first girl, the Ada of the family (by two minutes). As Yagazie grew older, she started to look more like Mama, less like me—her twin: her hips grew fuller, her face smoothened to rival Mama's, but what pleased and annoyed Mama most was that Yagazie acquired her stubbornness. Yagazie and I looked nothing like Papa. Mama said she thanked God every day for this because nine months was a long time to carry two babies and have them look like someone else.

The house is empty now. Papa is in Onitsha. He was here yesterday. He had bought a car from Porto-Novo and driven it into Lagos. "The corrupt officials at Lagos port would have kept me waiting for months!" he complained to Mama on the phone. They spoke Igbo to each other—a language he would pretend not to know when he turned to speak to Yaǵazie and me.

My food grows cold. I walk outside to the balcony and face the lagoon. I wonder what the September night sky sees when it looks down on earth. If it sees Yagazie as she was last year, here where I stand, smoking weed for the second time after she had come from the shrine, she had turned to me and said: "Sis, Olioma, we have to take pictures, just the two of us, abi? All you do is write poems. You don't dance with me. Pictures we can take together."

We went to the beach the next day. We carried a camera. It was during our school holidays. Papa and Mama had traveled. We left the house without telling them and took a danfo to Lekki. While I was so afraid, Yagazie was excited. She loved the thrill of doing the wrong thing. Papa had forbidden us from ever using a danfo. He feared we would enter a one-chance bus like our poor uncle Ikenna, or, worse still, we would be kidnapped. But even if he found out, he could only be angry at Yagazie for a few hours. Whenever we did something wrong, she stood in front of me while we were being reprimanded silently. When it was over, she would turn to me and say with authority: "Don't listen, Olioma! Some of these grown-ups sef, They don't know what they are saying." And she would drag me to another mistake as if the only wrong we did was to get caught.

An okada took us to the entrance of Elegushi Beach. Two beach boys immediately swarmed around us: "Madams, say you wan place to sit down?" they asked, directing us to the restaurants beside the beach. "Idiots! Get away! You only want moni!" Yagazie shut them up with a barrage of insults. She pulled me towards the beach forcefully, breaking into a run. I was behind her, struggling not to sink in the sand. We passed the shoreline. The water caressed our feet, wrapped itself around us, and then let go, like a lover motioning their beloved to a dance.

I went and changed into a bathing suit. Yagazie didn't bother. She only removed her shoes and left them underneath a parasol. We stood together and spread out our arms to the sea. Water soaked the hem of Yagazie's yellow dress. We walked into the sea, up to where the water reached our thighs. It was as far as we ever went. We never swam; we didn't know how to swim. We liked how the wind blew, how the waves beat against the shore, and how when we breathed deeply, time slowed, and the waves acquired a subtle, quiet feeling, as though beneath them, there was a palimpsest on which all of history was being written.

We set up the camera timer to take pictures. After we finished, we went and sat on the edge of the promontory. Yagazie rose. The black rocks we sat on were too uneven for her to dance on. Instead, she twirled her fingers and motioned her hands, moving with the waves. I took out my poetry book and wrote down what the sea said about her dancing.

Clouds formed above us. Evening was approaching; we needed to leave. Yagazie looked at me; she slanted her eyes and smiled. I knew we thought the same thought, as sisters do sometimes, and we almost, almost, said the same thing at the same time: "Sis, today is the best day of my life."

***

My dreams tell me rain is the presence of grieving clouds weeping. If true, Lagos today must be the saddest place on earth.

A raindrop falls on the window. I follow its trail with my finger until it disappears into the sill. Grey morning light filters in through silver droplets. Steamers move across the lagoon. I add creamed milk to my tea. A seashell Yagazie and I collected to decorate the dining table. I raise it to my ear and hear the sound of the sea, and Yagazie is trapped in it. Today is the day she died: a day I now use to number the rest of my days.

I walk back to my room and open the closet. I still only use half of it; the other half is empty; Yagazie still uses it: death is, after all, only the escape of spirits trapped inside bodies. That half calls itself her name sometimes. Her clothes are in a suitcase in a corner of our bedroom. Mama organized them to give away, but she ended up crying and couldn't move them any farther. The suitcase has the yellow dresses she liked to wear, her cardigans for when she was cold, and the ugly berets we wore at school. She liked wearing them because she said they made her look like she was about to release an Afrobeats album. The photographs we took together are all arranged neatly at the top. We printed and kept them. All our photographs were self-portraits: they were an expression of how we saw ourselves in different places. There are photographs of us lying on the grass at the playground in school. One of us is at the tennis court on our estate. One of us at The Jazzhole, with vinyl records and books in the background. My favorite one is one of us at the beach, where we are almost falling in laughter, our heads merged. These photographs capture the time we spent together. But what's the use of holding time in a photograph when you can't go back to it?

I close my eyes, and the world becomes dark inside me. A key turns downstairs. Taiwo always opens the door with ferocity. She lives on the mainland, in Surulere. It's Saturday. She never used to come on Saturdays. Papa asked her to come and keep an eye on me after Yagazie died. Sometimes, I wonder if he knows me at all. If he did, he would know all the wrong things I have done are because of my sister. Nowadays, my life is a bore. I am only waiting to write my WAEC next year. I want to become a poet. When I tell Papa that, I am sure he will collapse first. Yagazie and I were to tell him together that she wanted to be a dancer. She wouldn't have cared what Papa said or thought, and Papa would have assumed both of us didn't care.

My phone rings. It's Mama calling. When I answer, her voice rises over the hum of pouring rain. A breeze merges with it, and she sounds short of breath.

"Mommy, where are you?"

"I went to buy airtime to call you."

We both pause. I want to ask why she is still in Enugu after all this time. I walk downstairs, the phone in my ear. Taiwo cuts yam in the kitchen. She sings a familiar song. Mama's breathing is heavy. A car hoots. On the balcony, raindrops fall on my sweater. I tap on the railing and think of falling.

"I asked Taiwo to make you pounded yam and egusi," she says and laughs. She knows it was my favorite food as a child, Yagazie's, too.

I hear Mama struggle with her thoughts. She wants to tell me something.

"Olioma, can you believe your cousin Emeka is a Yahoo? He was arrested yesterday in Ikeja. He's been telling your auntie he's making home videos. Now she has been here crying since last night.

"Up Nepa! Up Nepa! Up Nepa!"

"Mommy, are you with someone?"

"No, Olioma, those are children. The lights are back. They had taken them for two days."

"Mommy, when are you coming?"

"Olioma, we will talk later. Right now, eat your food," she says and hangs up.

Mama blames herself for Yagazie's death. However, I am the one who should feel guilty—I was with her that afternoon—but I don't. I only feel sad and angry that Yagazie left me alone. On this day last year, we were in our parent's bedroom, searching for photographs of us when we were younger. Mama was in the parlor. Papa was away. They never liked anyone being in their room, so Yagazie and I had to be fast. As we searched, we found an old photograph of our parents before we were born. Mama was holding a baby, a son. Next to the photograph was a birth and death certificate. He died when he was six months old.

Yagazie was angry that Mama never told us about our brother. I, on the other hand, wouldn't have wanted to know. She rushed down with the picture, her face red with rage. I was behind her, escorting her anger and our overdue sadness.

"Mommy, you didn't tell us we had a brother!" Yagazie screamed at her. I had never seen her like that. She was always honest, even if her words were sometimes brutal, but never disrespectful.

"Who told you to go through my things? So you mean to say now, because you have small breasts like these, you can talk to me how you want?"

"Mommy, it doesn't change that you didn't tell us."

Mama rose from her seat. I felt the sound of the news channel she was watching reduce, even though she hadn't turned it down. She pointed an accusatory finger at Yagazie. "Eeh, so nowadays you talk like a hollow drum! There is something wrong with you—with the two of you! Don't think I don't know that you have been going to the beach without permission. Those pictures in your room are evidence. I was not born yesterday!"

"Mommy, so you also entered our room without asking—"

Mama slapped Yagazie before she could finish. I stepped back in shock. Mama never hit us at all. She turned to me and said: "Olioma, one day, this sister of yours will get you in trouble." Yagazie stared at me through balancing tears, her eyes accusing me of betrayal. I was certain she thought I was ingratiating myself to our mother. "I will tell your father you have become spoiled."

"Come, Olioma," Yagazie said. I followed her; I wanted her approval more than I was afraid of Mama's anger. She led me up the stairs. We picked up the camera and my school bag. When we went down again, Mama was still seething; she was telling Taiwo about how annoyed she was. Yagazie looked at our mother, insolence in her eyes. She opened the door. "Where are you going? Olioma! Yagazie! Come—"

We left the house. We raced each other down the stairs, our footsteps echoing in the sound of our mother's rage. We thought Mama might use the lift and find us on the ground floor, but she didn't. And when we burst into that day's sun, we felt we could do anything we wanted. "Olioma, don't worry; let's go to the beach. When Papa comes, he will be on our side."

We got to Elegushi an hour later. There were so many people that day. An event was due to happen later in the evening. It was rumored the oba was going to attend. The gateman was turning people away, but he let us through because he had seen us there many times before. The water was beautiful that day. It glistened like pearls. The sea breeze swept over our faces and became caught in our hair. We abandoned our usual spot at the promontory and walked along the shoreline, listening to the waves. We wrote our names in the sand and took photographs. Afterwards, we talked about the brother we never met. "He was probably an obanje sis," I said.

"I don't like hearing those traditional things, Olioma," she said. "I'm annoyed Mommy didn't tell us anything, and yet she wants to know everything about us." She untied her hairband, and as she wound it back, a braid fell off. She gave the braid to me, and I coiled it around my finger.

"Olioma, look!" She pointed to tourists not far from us. They were playing music and dancing on the shoreline. "Let's go there."

"No." I shook my head. I didn't want to get into the water that day. I hadn't carried a change of clothes.

"Okay, let me go. I'll come back." I watched my sister. She didn't know any of the tourists, but she knew how easily she interacted with them and how easily they laughed when she said something. She stepped into the water. She moved her waist and then her arms and legs, showing them how to dance on water. Water splashed around her in miniature rainbows against the sun, and they clapped for her. I took out my book to write a few lines.

Beauty dances in the shape of a water goddess
It leaves its shy half on shore
With portraits and a promise of return...

The light grew darker on the page I was writing on. Waves crashed loudly on the promontory. And then, someone screamed.

I looked up from my book.

Yagazie was nowhere.

The tourists she had been with were frantic. One was rushing out into the ocean, another was calling out to one of the fishermen, and another was running towards the lifeguard post. The waves were growing stronger. Out in the sea, I saw a hand calling for help. "Yagazie! Yagazie!" I screamed as I ran towards the water. Before I got to the shoreline, her hand was gone. The braid I held was the only thing left of her.

***

The rain slows to a drizzle. I want to go to the sea, where Yagazie drowned. I want to be with her today. I pick up my bag, some money, and our camera. "Olioma, where you dey go?" Taiwo asks me as I leave. "Oga will kill me if you go."

"I'll be back soon. I won't bring you wahala."

"What of food?"

"Don't worry, I'm coming."

As I walk towards the bus stop, I see Jamal, the boy I like. His father is a military man, a Fulani from Zaria. Jamal is tall and svelte, and even though he is handsome, I wonder why I wanted him so much.

I told Yagazie about him one day. We were in the kitchen. I was eating a mango above the sink. Its juice dripped down my arms and jaws, and the mango fibers showed as I ate. "Olioma, if that boy, Jamal, knew you ate mangoes like this, he would never talk to you again," Yagazie said.

"Sis, come on now, tell me, how somebody kisses? I want to kiss him, but I'm afraid I'll embarrass myself. He'll think I don't know anything. I know you've done it."

"It's easy; you do it like you see in movies."

"How now? Show me step by step. Use your hands."

"Olioma, you're wasting my time. Close your eyes."

"How will I see—"

"Do you want to learn or not?"

I nodded.

"Close your eyes and open your mouth a little."

I closed my eyes. Yagazie held onto my neck; she raised my chin and pressed her lips onto mine. She moved her hands and clasped my face; her tongue made a motion around my lips; she lingered for a moment and then let go. "That's how you kiss someone."

I move away from the road, unfurl my umbrella, and hide behind a building. He passes, and I breathe out. Our romance didn't go anywhere; after he and I kissed, Yagazie died, and I have been avoiding him since.

I arrive at the bus stop. A danfo stops, a keke stops, and finally, an okada. The driver, conductor, and rider motion for me to enter. I try to move my legs. Nothing. I tried again. Nothing. A strong wind blows. My umbrella slants. Raindrops turn spots on my sweater, a darker shade of green. They give up on me and avert their attention to other pedestrians. Yagazie would mock me for my failed attempt at disobedience, and then we would laugh together. I turn to walk back to the house. Suddenly, I stop, and tears flood my eyes.

***

School today is a chore. The English teacher reads out Okigbo's "Heavensgate" to us in a drawl. I sit at the back, writing my own verses. The sun increases in brightness. When the mid-morning bell rings, the whole class stirs awake. I go to the playground. The girls who used to be Yagazie's friends walk towards me. The three of them are in a different stream of our SS3 class. "Olioma, why can't you be more like your sister?" one of them, the tall one, says. I don't answer because it's already a stupid question. I was her twin. Didn't we look the same?

"I don't mean it like that. It's only that we miss her. We know you're different. We like you too, but you don't talk to us. You haven't talked to us in a year." I look at them, but I can't bring myself to say anything. A truth is being revealed to me: that I have been afraid of navigating the world without Yagazie.

The tall girl is annoyed at my silence. She starts to speak again.

"I'm sorry, I need to leave." I collect my bag from class and walk towards the school gate. The security guard is asleep, failing at his daily task of watching the day end. As I leave, I hear Papa's reproach accompanied by Yagazie's praise of my truancy. At home, I find Taiwo and Papa. He is in the parlor, on the phone with someone. He tells them how the elders in our ancestral home want him to take a title. When he sees me, he turns.

"What is wrong, Olioma? Why are you not in school?"

"Papa, it's girl issues. I don't feel well." I look straight at him, hoping that I look sick enough. If there is something Yagazie taught me, it's how to lie to our father: he does not like to hear about women's bodies at all. He calms down. I walk up to my room, and he goes back to his conversation: "If they were to build an inland port in Onitsha, the East would be far."

I spread out all the photographs Yagazie and I took at the beach on the bed. In all of them, we are facing the camera, the sea is behind us, and our arms are around each other. Yagazie is in her yellow dresses, while I'm in different clothes in each one. In some, we are smiling and laughing; in others, we are pouting and flashing the peace sign. I cut them into halves and put the side she appears inside my bag. I have decided to leave pieces of her in the places we used to go. I change my clothes and hurry downstairs. I lie to Papa that I need painkillers, and he gives me money. When I leave the house, I don't worry about what he will think when I get back in the evening.

I board a danfo. The sky is clear. Lagos is yellow. Today, it feels like a painting of a young man alighting from a bus station on his way to play football at dusk.

"Everybody know say na tiff Buhari tiff election from Atiku! We know say na bribe election tribunal! Omo, dis contri no dey go any wia o!" the man in front of me argues.

We pass the toll and enter Lekki.

I reach the beach at four. As I pay the entrance, I notice the security guard we know seated in an abandoned keke. He bolts up as if he has seen a ghost. Granted, it's my first time here in a year, and he probably thinks I am Yagazie. There are only a few people on the beach. Suya is being sold on the side where tourists crowd. The promontory Yagazie and I sat on has been sealed off with red tape around it. A child runs towards me and brings joy for a few minutes before her mother catches up to her and leads her away. When I turn to my right, I notice a shipwrecked oil tanker—*MT Anuket Emerald*. Next to it are three fishermen cleaning their boats.

I walk towards one of the fishermen.

"I want to go for a boat ride. How much is it?" He tells me. "What happened to the oil tanker?"

"Them tell us, say the ship dey go another side wey far from hia, but say the captain no fit control arm again, say the steering broke. Na so the ship come dey come dey come until e reach sand. All of us see am; me, I no dey hia, but all of us we see am. Na so oil dey commot like water. Thank Papa God, say nobody die." He prepares his boat. His muscles gleam in the sun. His feet form footprints on the black sand around the shipwreck. "Ma, get in."

"Make sure you go fast," I tell him. The boat hums to life. The waves make it sway. It parts the sea, unfolding only slightly the water that hides history, hurt, and Yagazie. Clouds begin to form. We leave the shoreline towards the horizon, the opening of a portal to another endless sea. I open my bag. As the water splashes behind us, I let go of the half-portraits. They fly in the air and fall into the water. The boat moves fast; I become the wind, the wind that merges with the sea.

The Way We Bend

1

When you arrive at Entebbe airport, the customs official in a white shirt and navy blue suit pushes a hand through the tiny window and gathers your passport. As soon as he opens it, he glances at you and says, "American, hmm."

"*African* American?" you say.

"Same difference," he says with a smug smile, stamps it, and tosses it back to you. "Next!" he shouts.

You stride to the baggage carousel just in time to see your two large bags popping up. You drag them outside and hail a taxi.

Deep inhale. The crisp freshness of morning air tastes like pure coconut water on your tongue. You see two elderly women talking to each other while they sweep the street with short brooms. Their heads are covered with bright orange scarves. You wonder how they don't trip over their floor-length dresses with square necklines, short puffy sleeves, and big sashes tied below the women's waistlines.

Suddenly, the sun appears as though to greet you. "Lovely," you say, beholding its bright red and golden rays dancing on the hilltops. You've seen images of African sunrises and sunsets in movies and books, but not this spectacular sight that makes your heart leap. You're so entranced that you don't hear what your driver says. Everywhere you look, the land is swathed in lush green. An abundance of avocado and mango trees laden with fruit sway amid the tall eucalyptuses and short acacias. Fruit sellers on the roadside move with baskets of ripe pineapples and tomatoes, stopping now and then to peer inside the windows of parked cars. You roll down your window to smell the air and adore the small, neat houses with tiled roofs hemmed in by luxuriant banana plants.

It's a bit chilly, but you like that the breeze refreshes you. You're in the Pearl of Africa! The idea to travel to this corner of the world possessed you after you did your DNA test and then watched movies featuring large families and communities holding ceremonies by the campfire, dancing, drumming, and eating meals together from the same tray; elders smoking pipes; and calling everyone brother or sister. Even the elephants looked cheerful, eating amarula fruits. You saw what was possible—a happy life elsewhere. Now, you can't wait to get to your room, call your brother in Lincoln, Nebraska, and tell him about your first impressions.

2

The taxi drops you off outside Dag Hammarskjöld Postgraduate Hall in Makerere, where you'll reside. A group of African students in the quad see you struggling with two samsonites and a carry-on duffel strapped to your back.

"This one is a settler," you hear one of them say, followed by laughter.

The custodian walks you to Room D4 and lets you in, but what you always remember is that he hands you the key without breathing a word and goes on arranging files in cabinets in alphabetical order. You climb the stairs, open the door, and welcome yourself inside.

3

With time, you introduce yourself to other international students from South Africa, Burundi, Kenya, Rwanda, Tanzania, India, China, Canada, Australia, Germany, Sweden, and Japan who have stayed from two weeks to five years. Some keep returning, never quite completing their research. Maybe, like you, they long to make Kampala their new home. Your next-door Japanese neighbor, Hinata, tells you she has shelved her first incomplete thesis on U.S. Military Engagement in Africa to begin new research on China's colonial interests. Chinese money has bought some islands off the shores of Lake Victoria, parts of the national forests, banks, and lately, infrastructure—roads and the airport. With a nervous laugh, Hinata adds that she's not yet figured out what really tickles her. Later, you hear rumors that she's prolonged her stay because she's a spy; she's fallen in love with the land, the weather, and the people; she's confused... What should I believe?

When you stroll through Wandegeya market near campus, vendors insist on calling you Mzungu—white—even when you tell them you're Black. You wonder if they've not seen Africans who look like you. Granted, when you stand before the mirror, which you've done a thousand times even before arriving in Kampala, you're struck by how, like your white mom, more than your brown dad, your complexion is. Strangely, your mother's relatives in Lincoln don't think you're white enough, and here, you aren't black enough.

Most evenings, the golden hour finds you on your fourth-floor patio, taking in the city's rolling hills. It pleases you to watch the men leaving Mulago Hospital, heading home, and entering bars or grocery stores. Sometimes walking hand in hand with the ladies or just alone. You see the legendary tall, broad, and ebony with milk-white teeth and belly laughs; then the slender and graceful ones—

brothers of Osiris walking with their heads held high; and king-size too—monumental. They make you gasp, not believing how they can be so large and agile at the same time. They remind you of your friend in college, Melissa, who dropped out to follow an African prince she'd met on a dating site. You never actually saw the 'prince', but now you imagine him in all the shapes and textures of these men. They speak several languages, and so you decide to immerse yourself in Swahili, Luganda, and Runyankole. Those who laugh at your broken sentences, you ignore. You keep trying until you're able to make conversation.

4

One day, you call a taxi in Luganda, and your smile competes with the sun.

"Olyota Ssebo?" you greet the driver. "Ngenda mukibuga eh Kampala. Mekka?"

"Speak to me in English, Mzungu. I understand English," he says.

Deflated, anger burns your face. As you edge closer, you do not see the pothole that bruises your big toe. "I am not a Mzungu," you scream at him. "I am Black."

"Ha! Oyo mulalu," one of the pedestrians passing by says to the driver. "Are there no mirrors in her house?"

"I am not insane!" you shout and launch into a history lesson—migrations of your black ancestors, your forefathers stolen from Africa, four hundred years of slavery, and your love of Africa so intense...

The pedestrian, amused and surprised at your knowledge of the language, brushes you off all the same. He moves closer to the taxi and starts chatting with the driver. It's like you don't exist. You're invisible. You turn and jump into the first matatu that appears.

Nearing the town center, you give the conductor a two-thousand-shilling bill, expecting him to deduct the trip's fare and give you the balance. After every passenger disembarks, the conductor says you've paid the trip's cost.

"Mpa sente zange," you insist.

He laughs and switches into Runyankole with the driver.

"Reka kunyiba," you challenge him.

He stares at you and finally concedes.

"Gyenda," he waves you off as you open your handbag and drop the coins inside. "Ogu noshanga nimbega," he mumbles so that only the driver can hear.

"I am not a spy," you say, with the full force of a riled-up woman.

You walk to the coffee house near the Grand Imperial building and order a double cappuccino. The waitress brings your coffee. Later, when she sees you fanning yourself with your left hand, she returns to your table with a paper fan. "My son makes them," she says, smiling. But you're too frazzled to exchange pleasantries.

Discomfort settles in your belly, and from then on, life becomes an uphill task. You always loop back to this moment in your effort to establish when things started to spiral out of control. Sometimes, when everything gets blurry, you shake your head and consider what to believe. You tell yourself that during your stay in Kampala, nothing strange happened. But once in a while, you retrieve what seems like events and images that brought you to your shadow.

5

You keep up with classes even as your joy runs out. When you greet your peers in managerial psychology, their smiles look plastic, as if they're merely stretching their jaws. They don't make eye contact. They seem tired or anxious to get back to reading their textbooks or opening laptops. You resort to sitting at the back of the room, where you can see everyone. Out of nineteen students, two may be your father's age. The ceiling light shines on their balding spots, and patches of gray hair on the sides of their heads give you the impression of a highway in the middle of winter, with gray trees on two sides of the road.

Before class starts, the older women in tight blue jeans and heavy make-up chat up their agemates, who prefer to banter with the young ladies tossing their braids every which way or running their fingers through curly bangs, cornrow plaits, straight perms, and wavy purple hair.

It amuses you—the world upside down—you wanting to fit in and feeling disregarded, the older women trying to engage their fellows, and dismissive younger women giggling at the older men.

Akello enters, huffing and puffing. She sits next to you and immediately opens her laptop, her wispy bangs dripping oil on the keyboard. That's when she turns to you and asks if you have any tissue. Chemical smells tell you she's come straight from the salon. Barbara's hair in front of you has a chestnut tint that reminds you of Beyoncé. The young men's heads, by comparison, are plain. Most are shaved, a style that's apparently in vogue and is popularly called Shaolin because it resembles monks' haircuts at Shaolin Temple. Only Thambo from South Africa has long and tidy dreadlocks. You pull your journal out of your rucksack and start drawing heads.

Professor Wakabi is late, as usual. You wonder what his excuse will be this time: Weather. Errant kids. A sick wife. A dead in-law… His list is endless.

Finally, the professor walks into the classroom. "Traffic is unusually terrible today," he says, removing his glasses. He quickly connects his laptop to a projector and displays a PowerPoint presentation on *The Future of Work*. On the left side of his screen is a conceptual framework demonstrating a traditional management style, and on the right is the new flexible model. "You may have all the data," he says, "but you won't succeed if you don't learn and actively participate in teamwork, team performance, and team measurement. While the challenge is no longer technical know-how, individuals and organizations must acquire emotional IQs to adjust and move from traditional command-and-control leadership to innovative cultivate-and-coordinate styles. This calls for new competencies, new mindsets, and management methods that place a high demand on self-organizing participatory, people-centered approaches. Are there any questions so far?"

None.

"Good. Let's have presentations."

When it's your turn to present "Global Networking" as an integral aspect of *The Future of Work*, you put on the wall your first two flipcharts—the research background, followed by the problem statement. You should read the background first.

"Pause!" the professor shouts before you proceed to the problem statement. "Class, what do you think?"

Thambo puts up his hand and says, "Her background lacks rigor. It's all jumbled. I think she's confusing global networking with globalization."

Akello speaks next, "There's really no problem in her problem statement."

"I haven't even read her statement," Wakabi says. "There's just too much noise in your background, young lady." He shifts uneasily in his chair and scratches his thick Afro hair. "You have not done enough reading, young lady. You still have cobwebs in your head, but I'll make a scholar out of you. Read more, then write with precision and clarity. Next!"

You slump into your chair. For the rest of the class, you observe how the stained, off-white walls don't match the refurbished concrete flooring. You're the first to walk out when presentations come to an end. You take slow, unsure steps.

6

You're hungry for conversation, so you call your father. He tells you he's had an equally draining day in court. "Just come back home," he says sharply, his razor voice cutting through your frustration and making you shudder. The thing you like and hate about him is his direct and confident manner. Wouldn't it be nice, just this once, to be indulged? He's often told you in his cutthroat, lawyerly voice that you're too nice. That the world is fiercely competitive. Iron sharpens iron. Your brother thinks he's badass, but to you, he's a ruthless rascal. You consider calling your mother, but in retrospect, picture yourself caught between a rock and a hard place as you weigh up your parents.

7

When you sleep, in contrast to the day's disappointments, you dream io color—a flock of chickens cackling joyfully with two cockerels. Their feathers a spectrum—deep blues and greens interspersed with bursts of red, oranges, and yellows like poppies mixed with marigolds. As you move to the middle of the hedge separating you from the chickens, their iridescent black feathers turn to deep purple. One of the cockerels dances towards you, and a surge of joy jolts you awake.

You forget the sepia gloom of the previous day. The chickens give you hope. You ache to see your life in color but feel like an invisible and spiteful veil stands between you and the others. But in this moment, your mind brims with beautiful images. What's more, the chickens' fellowship inspires you to go to church.

8

On a Sunday, you wear a long, black skirt and red blouse, comb and hold your curly hair in a tight coil. You adorn your neck with red beads and matching earrings, put on Masai sandals and tie the straps across your ankles. You brush your eyebrows with an old toothbrush and apply gloss to your lips. Lastly, you grab a Kikuyu bag and walk into one of the Pentecostal churches on Wandegeya-Kampala Road. The singing and drumming summon you long before you even see the building. Once inside, you embrace the energy around you. You lift your hands like the rest of the congregants, and the music transports you back to your Grandma's Baptist church. You were little when she held your small hands in her large palms and swayed with you.

One of the ushers holding leaflets for guests and newcomers taps your shoulder and asks if you're born again. For a moment, you don't understand what he means. He asks again, loudly this time. You shake your head.

"Thank you for coming," he says, "but you must be born again to fellowship with us as a family."

You want family, too! The connection. The feeling. He gives you a flier, which you leave blank. You appear the next Sunday if only to be reunited with the memory of your grandma. She could be any of these people. The choir calls everyone to dance, and, ah, the song, Lord of the Dance, gets you! You rise. You know the chorus to The Dubliners' hymn by heart.

The usher recognises you and asks why you've not filled the leaflet. Could you give him your phone number? You hesitate, but to get rid of him, you comply. He leaves you in peace. However, when it's time for members to give prayer requests, he puts up his hand and asks the whole congregation to pray for you so that you become born again. Everyone stretches their hands towards you to claim your soul for Christ. You do not go to church again.

A torrent of calls and texts to evangelize you flood your simple Nokia— *Why do you harden your heart against the Lord? The scripture says, "For God so loved the world, that he gave his only begotten son, that whosoever believeth in him should not perish, but have everlasting life." Don't you want a life that will never die?* You block him.

The chasm between you and the rest of the people widens. You recall the first time you read *Wide Sargasso Sea* during your undergrad. You did not like it that much, but now, a profound appreciation of the book grows when it occurs to you that you have a lot in common with the main character's feelings of alienation. You feel left out by an intentionally cruel design, as if you carry the label of Cain on your forehead. You play a game—Name your fears. Pain? No. Death? Surprise, no. Loneliness? Loneliness. That's it.

For all that you know and do not know, you wonder whether you're giving off loneliness vibes. Who wants to be near that? The warmth of chickens that had rippled in you, allowing you to dream and walk in color, dissipates.

9

Your shadow emerges and introduces you to other shadows—that's one way to think of what happens next. For a while, you feel something like happiness. And you're not alone. A life with strangers similarly looking for joy takes form. Ones you meet several times in a dimly lit bar. Or maybe he gives you a ride home as you're coming out of the bar, and something happens in the car. The details are blurry. You're out on the street to get some cigarettes, and a stranger joins you. You're out in the alleyway to get some fresh air, and a stranger uses you. He throws the lowest bill at you, and you cringe at the thought of what he thinks of you. You shake your head and replay the scene over and over:

After the bar closes, the one you believe you'd like in daylight as you've begun liking him in the dungeon bar leans into your ear and hums. Something about love being a cigarette. *Starts with fire, goes in smoke, then ashes. Do I care to be a chain smoker?* You weigh the possibility, and a new conversation opens. He takes you home, turns on the lights, looks into your face, and smiles. A sweet, dreamy smile. Something about his eyes and lightness relaxes you. In the morning, you hear him humming in the shower, and you like it. You think of him as a hummingbird. He makes you toast and good coffee. You give him your number and hope he calls. While you don't see him the next night, you hold him in your mind like a good idea. You never see him again, and when, finally, it dawns on you that you've been ghosted, the specter of his presence remains and occupies you.

10

You're with child. Alarmed and shocked. You don't know what to do. You carry it through the first trimester but eventually decide not to keep it. Abortions are illegal. In your desperation, you search for answers online—Google chat. You type, "Tips on self-induced abortion. No judgment, please." You post your note.

Within seconds, judgment reigns.

You should have kept your legs closed.

God will not be pleased, and his wrath will consume you.

Don't be a fool. Go see a doctor.

Throw yourself down the stairs and shake a lot.

Don't be an idiot. There are effective drugs. Talk to a pharmacist.

Old school suggests nothing beats a good, old-fashioned hanger. Make sure you're completely drunk.

Work out. Better yet, ride a rollercoaster. If it doesn't upset the baby to come out, go for a confidential abortion. Don't deal with that shit by yourself. You could die.

Nauseated, you close the page.

11

You avoid everyone, including your classmates. As your skin stretches around you, you wish to hide inside it and disappear. This is so fucking surreal! You hope you're dreaming, a terrible nightmare that will end when you awake, but the body doesn't lie.

Sometime later, fired by Absolut Vodka, you take matters into your own hands. Then wait. You lose strength and blood, and when you attempt to walk to the shared bathrooms, the farthest your rubbery legs can reach is your balcony.

"Help!" you scream.

Hands carry you.

Your semiconscious mind follows the white robe, gathering scissors and gloves. The pain in your abdomen is an octopus crawling and stretching its tentacles, burning and spreading to your splitting head like a bush fire, boring a dark hole into your skull. Kill the pain, you whisper. The discreet doctor pumps morphine into your veins. You shut your eyes and drift into a black sea. You can't tell night from day. You don't know how long it takes, but ultimately, you come to, and the doctor says it's over. You open your eyes and attempt to rise. The wails of a baby ring in your ears, and you consider returning to the numb world. It's over, all right, but when does it end? You cover your ears with your hands, but you cannot silence the baby. When you tell the doctor of this new occurrence, he prescribes Prozac.

"Perfect," you say, sinking your head back into the propped-up pillow.

Hinata approaches your bed and begins rubbing your back, humming a sad and terribly beautiful tune. You burst into tears, and she kneads the base of your neck and shoulders, following the rhythm of your sobs. She stays with you until you're discharged.

12

A few of your classmates visit with a vase of white, pink, and purple dahlias. Thambo carries his guitar, and you ask if he can play. He takes it from its case and strums a few chords while you notice his long and slender fingers. His deep voice breaks into a cheerful melody that moves you. Meanwhile, Akello gives you fresh juice and a green nightdress with pictures of chrysalises below the neckline. She asks how you're doing, and you say so-so. After everyone leaves, she lingers.

You fold your arms across your chest, not sure how to interpret the turn of events.

Akello asks if you'll consider talking to a therapist.

You shrug.

She says she can talk to Isanda, her therapist. "He's really good," and if you want, she can help with making appointments.

"I'll sleep on it," you say, and before leaving, she says she'll be seeing you.

13

Akello accompanies you on all your visits and waits on a bench in the corridor. You sit facing Isanda and wonder if it's going to be a waste of money and time.

"Do you think I'll get better?" you ask him.

"Why don't we start with how you're feeling today?"

"Dead."

"And yesterday?"

"Dead."

"What about tomorrow?"

"Indulge me," you say and smile. It surprises you and feels good to relax the jaws. It does not take one session, but slowly, you consider how better you might feel if you were to release the weight of guilt. Something new and soft starts to sprout along the dark edges of bad feelings. But you're suspicious and cannot trust any positive emotions easily.

"You know," Isanda says one time, "you're not your thoughts."

"I've heard that before."

"Life breaks us all," he continues, "but many are made strong at the broken places."

"Hemingway said that."

"I'm glad you know."

"He committed suicide."

"Take the lesson, not the action."

"I get them: compulsive thoughts prompting me to end my life. And I'm afraid. I'm not ready to go back home because I don't want my family to see me in this state."

"You have a choice to love or judge your scars."

You inhale. "Is it that simple?"

"You tell me."

After you're done with your session, Akello walks with you through the narrow and crowded Biashara Street in Wandegeya. She pauses to greet her hairdresser while fruit sellers and clothes vendors address you: "Mzungu leta sente." You ignore them.

At Wandegeya's small gate to campus, you stop to buy roast maize. You dig your teeth into the corn, warm and sweet. You feel something unfinished and something else new coming into being simultaneously. Akello pats your arm and turns to go home. "Tomorrow?" Akello says, and you nod.

Ma felt frail and sweaty, but she held me like she would never let me go. At that moment, I felt fulfilled for managing to fill the vacuum left in her life by Adanne's demise, even though it left me emptier. I've gradually come to accept the responsibilities Adanne's death saddled on me. I kept clogging God's ears with her name, till I believed that God, tired of my disturbance, must have dragged her to her bosom, where no one would come for her.

Body Parts

I've taken to swimming early. Before sunrise, I drive down to Muizenberg and, in the dark, make my way to the edge of the ocean. People warn against swimming at dawn or dusk; it's feeding time for sharks. I take the risk. Life is full of risks anyhow.

When I was around twelve, my father tried to turn me into a swimmer. His colleague, also a doctor, coached his daughter into becoming a famous water ski champ. Karin Muir from Kimberley swam for South Africa overseas. Her father also pushed her and made her a champion. My father pushed her name at me. Perhaps I was his last hope for fame. He enrolled me in training at the municipal pool daily at five a.m. I hated the cold water, the icy mornings, the deep Olympic-sized pool, and the smell of chlorine. Like the underground parking basement at Pa's office, the depths terrified me. I imagined a shark coming from the shadows, tearing off my limbs. In the pool, I felt entombed. My arms flailed, my feet kicked, and my eyes blinded by the chlorine. The training lasted about a year, enough for the coach to improve my stroke but not my speed. Then, my father gave up on me and the training as suddenly as he'd become obsessed with it. It was about that time that he gave up on himself.

Perhaps, if I'd shown talent, he'd have gone on fighting, kept his head above water for longer, and survived. I had my tonsils removed around then, so I couldn't speak. I told him I was sorry I wasn't better at swimming. At home, with the doors closed, I could hear them arguing. "We want you, not money," Ma said to him. I didn't know yet what it felt like to be depressed, to see no end to the depths. I watched as my father fell and disappeared under dark waters.

I didn't swim again—not in municipal pools. Ma didn't like the boys I went out with, so I never took any of them home. I ran from her and the shadow of my father. I left school, moved to Johannesburg, and got a job. I found employment in a gift shop off Commissioner Street, *The Yellow Submarine*. I made raffia sandals with flower-power daisies. They cost nothing to make, but the shop sold them with no commission. I kept the music playing and chose my favorite sites: Creedence Clearwater Revival and The Fifth Dimension.

In that year without my father, the year I turned eighteen, I wandered the streets of Jo'burg as if I were doing laps in a pool again, up and down, in and out. I wanted to call out to him to watch me, but he was nowhere. Not in Commissioner, Rissik, Pritchard, Eloff, or Loveday Streets. I floated along pavements, breast-stroked past entrances to parking basements, crawled past newspaper vendors at every corner and beggars at traffic lights. I swam between the red city buses and morning traffic, veering between tsunamis of motorbikes and shoals of Yamahas and Suzukis. I told myself to keep brushing against death. It becomes a whisper, just a breath, and you can face anything. Sometimes, I was sure I saw him, my father, just ahead, turning a corner. I'd paddle, quickening my pace and my heart.

At lunchtime, I turned on my back, stroked across the Oppenheimer Gardens, and dove under the sculpted springboks, a vaulting arc, over the fountains. Signs on benches read "whites only."

Was he there reading a newspaper, invisible like those who weren't allowed in the inner city?

Once, I followed a man all the way down Anderson Street. I tapped him on the arm, but when he turned, he had the face of a stranger.

Near the building where I worked was a car basement like the one he'd parked in. The steep concrete ramp led down a slipway to dark waters. Once, I plunged down to see if his car was there—his black Mercedes 220—but there were only shadows.

Now, years later, I live in another city. I swim again—in the sea. Opaque, it hides the depths. I cannot see what's below the surface. False Bay is renowned for great white sharks, but I'm taking my chances. Recently, a pod of orcas arrived to prey on the sharks, ripping their livers right out. Three sharks beached on the sand and died there, their sides gaping holes.

In the dark, I swim out through the waves, as far as I dare, until the sea becomes flat. Then I turn and swim laps parallel to the shore. Up and down as if I'm in a swimming pool. I pause to catch my breath. Sometimes, I see him, my father, on the shoreline, holding up his hand, a specter.

But those days, when I walked the inner city of Joburg, it was as if I was swimming in a city submerged. I was a fish exploring underwater caverns, following the flickering lights of fluorescent fish. I knew the signs of the Coliseum, His Majesty's, the large letters of the department stores, and the flashing bulbs of Ster Kinekor. On Eloff Street, the red letters of the OK Bazaars lured shoppers. I'd swim right on by the open-mouthed store with its cheap smells of nylon and crimplene, its garish counters, and the Saturday girls from the south trying on lipsticks and bright green eyeshadow.

I'd continue up, past furniture shops, hairdressers, and barbers, up past Sterns and the dazzling diamonds, a girl's best friend, to the junction of Pritchard Street. The doors of John Orr's angled the corner. The smells of leather, Chanel No. 5, tweeds, linen, and lavender. There was a tearoom on the top floor. When we were all still together, Pa took us to the city to shop and go to the cinema. Ma always made a stop at John Orr's. We traveled up by lift, the operator announcing the floor. First floor: Ladies' Wear. Second floor: Haberdashery, Textiles. There were rolls of fabric for new dresses and patterns from *Vogue* or *Simplicity*. Fifth floor: Tearoom.

We'd begin with a platter of sandwiches and cakes, pots of tea. Pa would leave us to shop while he went on other business. He loathed shopping. Once, he was late to fetch us. He'd been to the cinema, *Khartoum*. We'd seen *The Sound of Music* and *My Fair Lady* on previous visits, but now he'd gone alone.

"How could you?" I asked.

"It was a war film," he said. He described red sands, desert ships, the camels, and blood that flowed. He wanted to reminisce about his war, the desert in North Africa, the tanks, the fighting, and seeing body parts blown off by other soldiers in his regiment. Captured at Tobruk, he was entombed in the bowels of a ship sailing across the sea to Italy, torpedoed a few miles off the coast.

It's dark when I arrive at the beach. Soon, it will be winter, and sharks will be more abundant. I park near the Super Tubes slides and lock the car. I make my way in the dark between the fence of Super Tubes and the law enforcement office; there's no moon. The gulls are white stars swimming in the night sky. The pavilion looms ahead, its concrete floor a reef of the vagrants that sleep here in bags made of newspaper. In summer, they're up and gone by now, but in winter, they lie in—depending on how much tik they've had.

I don't want to trip over them; my bare feet register when I leave the tarmac and touch the sand. The sand is wet and cold from the high tide, and I stumble. I reach out to feel the concrete support. There is a glow from the water, the white foam tips over the falling waves, and I make my way to the ocean.

I swim out beyond the breakers, swim parallel to the shore. My hair is still damp and smelling of brine. I walk from the beach past where the bergies are still huddled. I cross at the traffic lights and make my way past the parking garage to the station.

It's not yet eight a.m. I'm on the train, crossing the peninsula, stopping at stations: Lakeside, Retreat, and Diep River. Vendors sell fish dipped in batter, whole roe fried like a sausage. Each time the door opens, the smell enters along with the passengers. The compartments fill up; we're sardines, a bait ball. There is no inspector to check Metro Plus cards.

I sit with other women, my purse secured under my jacket. We could be picked off from the edges.

The lights of the suburbs are bright, and we can see right into people's homes. Fishbowl living. More people enter the carriage; five squashed up on a bench meant for three. I hum "Yellow Submarine" until the train stops in the city.

I walk from the station to where I work on St. George's Street. Night eyes watch me; bottom feeders, sea dragons down every alleyway—there's no St. George or Neptune. I have to look out for myself.

I nod to the homeless in the alley alongside my office building. They're rolling up their mats, packing their scant belongings into garbage bags to stash behind the bins at the end of the alley. One of the homeless youths has acquired a small black kitten. His eyes are as jade green as the kitten's. He is in deep conversation with it, talking in soft swishing sounds.

"Morning," I say.

"Môre," they say—or "Molo," depending on the language they speak. There's a van idling nearby. It's rounded on the ends, the shape of a submarine—black with tinted windows. Then, it drives off.

Back then, in the other city, I'd see the ghost of my father lurking in doorways. I'd look for him in Rissik Street, down Commissioner Street, in Loveday Street. Sometimes, I saw him walking ahead, black suit and white cuffs of his shirt, as his arms swung. He'd stride up Anderson Street, and I'd try to catch up. Back then, the streets of

Joburg were filled with ghosts; most of the citizens were forced out to eke out a living in the shallows.

Now, here swimming in Cape Town, I wonder if mad Adamastor will send his sea dragon, Nkanyamba. I am a fish out of my depths. Will Nkanyamba net me? At the station, fat pigeons scratch for crumbs. I hear a high screech. High up on the skyscraper is a falcon. Hunting the fat pigeons.

The van is there again, idling alongside the alley like a shark. The bergies are awake. Today, they're arguing. "Where's Sam the Man?" I ask. Jade is singing to his kitten; I recognise the tune: Herman's Hermits. Surely, Jade's too young to know it. Perhaps his parents sang it to him when he was a kitten. No one responds.

"Where's Sam?" I ask again.

"They took him."

"Who?"

"You've been living alone with no Bell telephone," Jade answers.

It's Monday. Winter's holding off. I'm pleased for the homeless. They're usually slower after a weekend. But there's no one in the alley; only a few of their bags remain. As I pass the ramp to the basement parking, I see two men dragging someone into the depths: Jade. He's holding his kitten aloft, and it's flying through the air.

I hold my breath and slip down the ramp alongside the cold, gray wall. At the bottom, I peer around the corner. Shielded by a wall that houses the lift, I make my way to a metal storage container. Inside, it is narrow, hardly big enough for a child, but I squeeze in. A small red light glows. My own submarine. I curl up tight, my knees up against my ears. The red light pulses. It is like being in the womb again: the darkness, the red glow. Outside voices are dulled as though coming through water. There are mutterings, a drumming in my ears. Phrases could be a foreign language. Inside, the tiny red light throbs like blood coursing, like the blood that coursed through my mother, feeding me, nourishing me.

I wonder if this is how it felt inside Ma's tummy, securely curled up inside her. Safe there. Is the deep drone my father's voice, the thudding in my ears her heartbeat or mine? It becomes darker, and a shadow hovers. Is he the cloud across my stratosphere? Are his hands moving over her belly?

I am cramped, folded up like a seahorse, to survive. The slightest jerk could fling open the door and swish me out in a gush of bloody birth waters. I could drown here in this subterranean vault.

Did you see his shadow Ma? Did you look for him in the streets wondering? You saw his body, Ma. You signed the forms for his organs to be donated: his eyes, his kidneys, his heart. His brain was no more.

I'm far away now Ma, and yet I continually search for him. I see him clearly some days, follow him for miles up and down streets. He's in a coffee shop reading the paper or on a bus with a book.

Still folded up in this metal container, I smell the sea -brine in my hair. Did it smell like this inside your womb? Did you wonder who I was, did Pa? Did he hope for a boy? Would he have gone if I'd been a boy?

I peer out again. There's a vehicle; it's the van, a kind of ambulance. Completely black, no markings. The back doors are open, and the men who dragged Jade, the two thugs who manhandled him, lift him onto a table inside.

Jade, who is clearly unconscious now, is on a gurney, like an operating table, covered in a green cloth. Inside is a man in scrubs, a light, spotlighting the table. The man lifts Jade's hoodie and T-shirt, turns him onto his side, and makes an incision. A flash of steel, a metal dish, a kidney dish for a kidney. And then another.

My eyes work at absorbing what is happening. The organs are now in a cooler box, on ice, sealed. TJade is lifted off, taken by the two thugs, and placed into the boot of another car nearby. The van's door is closing, and both cars are driving off, up the exit ramp and out into the street. Different directions. I have to find someone to tell, go to the police.

When I swam in the sea in the early mornings, stroking long arms in the waves, I tried to forget about him. But with the black cat in Jade's arms, the alley woke the shadows again. My father was the doctor, who dealt in women's parts, slicing and splicing their bodies, pulling babies from within their dark waters. The light at the end of his examination table, the light he used, exploring the dark inner cavities. Women's body parts.

I look through the crack again. Someone is passing in front of the cupboard. If I'm expelled from my womb cave in a burst of blood, I will be in terrible danger. Perhaps my organs will be given away, too. If I am reborn in another country, what will I see? Will my eyes open to the hot deserts of Khartoum? Perhaps it will be the Himalayas; will I see the stars above in those heavens? And will I look for Pa there, too?

Will my eyes look down every alley, look at every man around forty years reading a paper, sitting on a train? Will my arms strike out in the waters of the Ganges as I swim across their width? Will my hair smell of its murky, pungent waters? And those funeral pyres on the steps, a thousand lights reflecting in the river, will I finally see my father again; his eyes in someone else's head, his body set alight and floating down the river to finally find the open ocean, the salty sea, the uterine waters of the world?

Author Biographies

Alex Nderitu

Alexander Nderitu is a Kenyan poet, novelist, playwright and critic. Some of his work has been translated into Arabic, Japanese, Chinese, Kiswahili, French, Swedish, Dholuo, Gikũyũ, and Czech. His poems have appeared in The East African Standard (Kenya), Ars Artium (India), My Africa, My City: An Afridiaspora Anthology (Nigeria), World Poetry Almanac (Mongolia) and the World Poetry Yearbook (China), among other publications. During the 2014 Commonwealth Games in Glasgow, Scotland, his narrative poem Someone in Africa Loves You represented Kenyan literature on Common via Commonwealth Postcard. It has since been translated into five languages. In 2017, Business Daily newspaper named Nderitu one of Kenya's 'Top 40 Under 40 Men'. In 2020, he was a finalist for the Collins Elesiro Literature Prize. In 2022, he took third place in the Share Africa Climate Fiction Awards. In 2023, he was conferred a 'Jury Award' in the Sahitto International Awards for Literature.

Nderitu is the Deputy Secretary-General of Kenyan PEN and a Regional Managing Editor for TheTheatreTimes.com.

Christine Coates

Christine Coates holds a Master of Arts in Creative Writing from the University of Cape Town. Her poems and stories have been published in various local and international literary journals. She has four collections of poetry: Homegrown (Modjaji Books, 2014), Fire Drought Water (Damselfly Press, 2018), The Summer We Didn't Die (Modjaji Books, 2020), and RED LETTER DAYS (The Explainer's Press, 2022). Her debut collection, Homegrown, received an honourable mention from the Glenna Luschei Prize. Poems have been included in Old Love Skin: Voices From Contemporary Africa by Mukana Press, Coming Home: poems of the Grahamstown diaspora 2019, and the Cambridge Contemporary Poetry Review 2002, Africa Focus. Her short stories have been short-listed and won prizes in several competitions: the Commonwealth Writers' Prize, and adda, the Commonwealth Writers' Journal. Other stories have been awarded and published in publications such as the Short.Sharp. Stories, the Short Story Day Africa, Long Live the Short Story, and the Kalahari Short Story Competition. A book of short stories, The Cat's Wife and Other Stories is forthcoming. Coates is sensitive to environmental issues and finds solace and inspiration in nature. She also has an interest in life-writing and the recovery of personal history through public and private imagery. She has an interest in life-writing or memoirs and the recovery of personal history through public and private imagery.

Dennis Mugaa

Dennis Mugaa is a writer from Meru, Kenya. He won the 2022 Black Warrior Review Fiction Contest, was shortlisted for Isele Magazine's inaugural Short Story Prize and was longlisted for the 2021 Afritondo Short Story Prize. His work has appeared in Jalada

Africa, Lolwe, Isele Magazine and Washington Square Review. He is the 2023/2024 Rajat Neogy Editorial Fellow, and he has a Master of Arts in Creative Writing from the University of East Anglia, where he was a 2021/2022 Miles Morland Foundation Scholarship recipient.

Mildred Barya

Mildred Kiconco Barya is a North Carolina-based writer and poet of East African descent. She teaches and lectures globally and is the author of four full-length poetry collections, including The Animals of My Earth School, published by Terrapin Books in 2023. Her prose, hybrids, and poems have appeared in New England Review, Shenandoah, Joyland, The Cincinnati Review, Tin House, Forge, and elsewhere. She's now working on a collection of creative nonfiction, and her essay, Being Here in This Body, won the 2020 Linda Flowers Literary Award and was published in the North Carolina Literary Review. She serves on the boards of the African Writers Trust and Story Parlor and coordinates the Poetrio Reading events at Malaprop's Independent Bookstore/Café. She blogs here: www.mildredbarya. com.

Gloria Mwaniga Odary

Gloria Mwaniga Odary (Minage) is a writer and educator from Kakamega, Kenya, currently pursuing an MFA in creative writing at the University of Memphis in Tennessee. In 2019, Mwaniga was awarded the Miles Morland Writing Scholarship, and in 2022, her story Boyi was awarded the inaugural African Land Policy Centre story prize and subsequently included in Finding Ground and Other Stories: ALPC Anthology of Short Stories on Land in Africa and in the Kenyan High School Curriculum. Mwaniga's fiction has appeared in The Johannesburg Review of Books, The Nation, The White Review, Munyori Literary Journal and Ebedi Review. Her nonfiction essay, A Few More Words About Breasts, was published by Isele Magazine in 2023. For over 10 years, Mwaniga published book reviews and author interviews in The East African and the Nation newspapers in Kenya. She has also published 11 children's books with Moran (E.A) Publishers Ltd and Longhorn Publishers. For eight years, she worked as a high school teacher of Geography and Business Studies. Mwaniga is an alumna of the Purple Hibiscus Creative Writing Workshop taught by Chimamanda Adichie.

Favour E. Ahuchaogu

Favour Ezienyi Ahuchaogu is shamefully addicted to two or maybe three things: her phone-cum-internet, fried yams and sweet potatoes, sappy romance novels and k-dramas, and sleep, in no particular order. She is a graduate of English and Literary Studies from the University of Nigeria, Nsukka. She currently works as a Sales and Marketing Executive with a Pharma-FMCG company but tries her best to never stop doing what she loves the most, which you guessed right, is writing. In 2021, Favour's "Daughter of the Soil" was shortlisted for the Ekonke Short Story Competition. That same year, she won the TWMN Prize for Young Female Writers (Short Story Category). Her story, "Of Weddings and Funerals", emerged second place in the ALITFEST21 Prize for Short Stories and "Fernweh" was shortlisted in 2022 for the Brilliant Flash Fiction Contest. You can also find her story "Love on Transit" in the 49th edition of The Muse.

Chioma Iwunze-Ibiam

Chioma Iwunze is a lecturer in Cornell University's Creative Writing program. When she isn't teaching an intro. to creative writing seminar and a first-year writing seminar titled Happiness in Short Stories, she is writing fiction, academic essays, experimental poetry and/or creative non-fiction. She is drawn to themes like maternal interiorities, immigration, mathematical research, and dance research. Her literary works have received several awards, including the Cecilia Unaegbu Prize for Fiction, the Voice of America Award for flash fiction, the James McConkey Master of Fine Arts Creative Writing

Award, and the David L. Picket '84 Summer Fellowship. A proud alumna of Cornell University's MFA in Creative Writing Program '23 and Chimamanda Adichie's Creative Writing Workshop, her works of literature have attracted the support of esteemed institutions like Fidelity bank, Goethe Institut, and FEMRITE. Creativewritingnews. com, is a non-profit educational platform she founded specifically to empower and nurture emerging writers. If you'd like to read some of her previous publications, scour the catalogs or forthcoming issues of Mukana Press Anthology 2023, Aster(ix) Journal, Ankara Press, Maple Tree Literary Supplement, Flash Fiction Press, Fiction 365, Ebedi Review Anthology, and various others. Currently, she is working on a novel that portrays the lives and struggles of a fractured immigrant family in a fictitious American town. Like her on Twitter via @ChiomaIwunze_ and follow her on Facebook via @Chioma Iwunze-Ibiam

NmaHassan Muhammad

A versatile writer, NmaHassan Muhammad writes both fiction and Nonfiction and across poetry, drama, radio play, children's stories, short stories and songwriting. He served as the Assistant Editor for Impact Magazine by NSBIREDA for one year. He was a two time secretary and former chairman of the Association of Nigerian Authors (ANA), Niger State branch. Born in Bida, he earned a bachelor's degree in Estate Management from Federal University of Technology Minna, professional certificates in Computer Engineering, Mass Communication, Facility Management and Post Graduate Diploma in Education.

Since taking writing seriously in 2020, NmaHassan Muhammad has won multiple scholarships including GrubStreet, Tin House Workshop, Highlight Foundation, Murphy's Writing, The Writing Barn, IWWG, a Fellowship from Ebedi International Writers Residency, and has been placed on shortlists and longlists including Sevhage Prize, African Writers Award, Wakini Kuria Prize, and

The Welkin Prize in which he also won the prize for Carer for an Adult Dependant. His work has been published in ANA Review, Kalahari Review, The Writers and Readers' Magazine, The Welkin Prize and elsewhere, including anthologies. When he's not writing, he's listening to Kira'a, watching movies and Nigerian comedians, or helping with changing baby Hamood's diaper or teaching three-year-old Fatima chess. He lives in Minna with his family, siblings and aged mother.

Okoronkwo Chisom

Okoronkwo Chisom is a first-class graduate of English Language and Literature. She is the winner of the Shuzia "Journey of the Soul" Poetry Contest 2023 and the Delyork Creative Academy Writing Contest 2021. She has been shortlisted in the Eriata Oribhabor Poetry Prize 2022, Africa Feminist Short Story Prize 2022 and the Vweta Chadwick Poetry Prize 2023. Her works have been published or are forthcoming in the Isele Magazine, New Man Gospel Magazine, PoetryColumn, Nigerian Review, Blue Marble Review, Icreative Review, Afrihill Press, Mukana Press, Lunar Journal, and elsewhere.

Delight Chinenye Ejiaka

Delight Chinenye Ejiaka is a fiction writer whose works focus on the African experience and history. She is an MFA candidate at the University of Nevada, Las Vegas. She was a finalist for the 2022 Frontier Global Poetry Prize. Her works have appeared or are forthcoming in Isele Magazine, What You Need To Know About Me anthology, Lee Review, Whale Road Review and Vindagua. Twitter @DEjiaka

Munashe Kaseke

Munashe Kaseke was born and raised in Harare, Zimbabwe and currently lives and works in Northern California. Tsoro is an excerpt from her debut short story collection, Send Her Back and Other Stories. Send Her Back and Other Stories is critically acclaimed, winning the following prizes, Anthem Award – Silver -Category:

Research and Publications, Foreword – Gold -Category: Short Stories, Next Gen Indie Book Awards – Finalist -Category: BIPOC, Reader Views – Gold Award and Global Award Winner – Africa - Category: Short Stories, Nautilus Book Awards- Silver - Category: Multicultural and Indigenous, Independent Press Award – Distinguished Favorite, Independent Publisher Awards (IPPY's) – Bronze - Category: Multicultural Fiction. You can follow her on Twitter @munashe_ kaseke